Tell Me What You
WANT
KNIGHTS OF TEXAS BOOK ONE

SUSAN SHEEHEY

AMEPPHIRE PRESS

Amepphire Press
Trophy Club, TX

eBook ISBN: 978-1947874008
Print book ISBN: 978-1947874022

Published in the United States of America

First eBook Edition: October, 2017
First Print Edition: November, 2017
Second Print/eBook edition, April 2019

Teaser
EXCERPT

Cassie caressed his chest in small circles with her fingertips. Renner's skin was smooth. She forced her fingers to stop and just focused on his heartbeat. Strong and steady.

His hand closed over her fingers and brought them to his lips. He kissed each one, slowly. Every touch made her heart skip.

"I know you're curious, Cassie." His voice, low and sensual, made the hairs on the back of her neck stand up.

If they weren't covered in darkness, he'd see her blush—the heat was in her cheeks. Because she *was* curious. Extremely. She didn't know if she was brave enough.

Brave enough to feel. To want.

To let go.

"You're in the driver's seat." Renner's words were honey across her cheeks. Warmth drifted across the single foot of space between them. Soothing, musky warmth. "I won't make any moves until you do."

A tremor slid down her spine. She took a shaky breath to settle her nerves. A tempting, red-horned devil sat on her shoulder, urging her to let go of her reserves and press her lips to Renner's. The haloed, sensible voice in her mind told her the last thing she needed was an opportunity for guilt in an already emotion-filled heart, over capacity.

Tightening her grip on his hand, she curled it under her chin. "Good night, Renner."

She felt him smile—rather than saw it.

"Sleep well, Cassie."

Novels By
SUSAN SHEEHEY

Stand Alone Novels

Audrey's Promise

Royals of Solana series

Prince of Solana

Jewel of Solana

Crown of Solana

Royal Wedding

Knights of Texas series

Tell Me What You Need

Tell Me What You Crave

Tell Me What You Want

Tell Me What You Feel

Sweet Escape series

Dry Spell

Hot Spell

Cold Spell

Dedication

To My Husband
My infinite source of love, and killer one-liners

Chapter
ONE

RENNER

"To the land of the living." Dorian tapped his beer glass to Renner's. The music blared throughout the club, and the deep bass pounded in his ears. The VIP section was the only thing separating him from the rest of the packed venue.

"And dumb ass luck," Renner said. He downed half his beer in a few seconds. The cold, bitter taste so welcome it turned nearly sweet on his tongue. His first sip in four months.

"No shit. You must be Irish."

He bit back a grimace. No, that was Glicker. Poor bastard.

The blonde bombshell on Dorian's arm whispered in his ear.

He grinned and gave the woman an eager nod. "Excuse me, gents." He followed her to the dance floor.

Renner couldn't remember her name, but her raven-haired friend hadn't stopped staring at him for the last thirty minutes.

She'd introduced herself as Gloria, and was on her third chocolate martini. She'd sidled up next to Riggs, his former Marine buddy and hay-blond cowboy for most of the time, but her attention was clearly focused on Renner.

He appreciated the fairer sex like any other red-blooded man, especially after the dry spell right before the accident, then elongated for four more months of recovery.

"So, Dorian tells me you've been out of commission for a while." Her sultry voice caressed the air with the music. And her come-hither gaze locked on his. "Occupational hazard?"

"Something like that." The gunshot wound and surgery scars prickled at the reminder. "Currently looking for a new job, now that I'm back on my feet."

"Are those feet up for a dance?" She rose, and extended her hand.

Renner slanted a smile at her, downed his beer, then stood to join her. For the next eight songs, she never let go of his waist. Except to squeeze his biceps or caress the short stubble his cheek. The minimal small talk was as pleasing as her flowery perfume. He appreciated her simple makeup and small frame that fit in his hands easily. No need for a weapon with this one.

After another sensual rhythm—purposely made to grind against someone—she lifted up on her toes, and kissed the tender skin on the side of his neck. "I have a room at the hotel across the street," she cooed into his ear. "Care to join me for a nightcap?"

A warm zing spread through his body. The assuming curve of her lips was unmistakable. And contagious.

He looked around the dance floor, but Dorian wasn't there. He'd moved to their VIP seats, where the blonde had draped her legs across his lap. The dark fuzz on his face and muscular arms twice the size of his own more than made up for his shorter stature.

Women were always drawn to the tattooed, bad-boy image. His gaze moved to Renner, with a knowing smile. He raised his beer to him from across the room with a wink.

There's my cue.

"Sure. Sounds fun."

The next morning, Renner woke alone. Not his first one-night-stand, but normally *he* was the one who left first. Although, he'd always at least said good-bye beforehand. As he stood to get dressed, he noticed an enveloped on the dresser. In neat feminine handwriting:

Renner, Thanks for an awesome night!

Stuffed inside was a bunch of bills.

What the hell?

Renner glared at Dorian and Riggs across the breakfast table at Sunny's Diner. His scrambled eggs and bacon with wheat toast went untouched. He tossed the thick envelope of cash on the table. "Is this supposed to be charity?"

Dorian chuckled, and took a bite of his oatmeal. "Hardly. Just a 'welcome back' gift."

"Tell me you didn't hire her for me."

Riggs threw him a smirk. "Other way around, pal."

He narrowed his eyes. "You lost me."

"We hired *you*, for her."

His mouth went dry. "No." His voice came out harsh. "I'm out of personal security. Give this back to her. She can find a bodyguard somewhere else." He stood to leave. "I thought I made it clear that life was over for me."

"Wait, Renner." Dorian grabbed his arm. "Not as a bodyguard. You were her *date*."

"What?"

His buddy sighed. "Technically, she was my date. But she asked if she could switch to you, because she liked your military look, and I agreed. The tip she left is all yours."

His heart stopped, and heat flooded his face. "She paid me for sex?" A few other patrons around them stared in their direction. Renner sat, and lowered his voice. "You made me a gigolo?"

"No," Riggs replied. "She paid you for your time and your company."

The taste still didn't sit well in his mouth.

He gulped his water.

"I didn't think you'd mind the gift." Dorian rubbed the

back of his neck. "Gloria's a regular of mine, and needed a night out. I invited her to this, and when she saw you, she asked to switch her time to you."

A regular?

"You're an escort?" His mind wouldn't wrap around that.

"No. I'm a Knight."

"What does that mean?"

His long-time friend reclined and rested his elbow on the chair. "Do you really want to know?"

Duane Wilkes tossed a wink at the waitress, and checked his Breitling watch. Never mind that his smartphone sat on the table with the time on bright display, but Renner admitted the man sported a nice accessory. Almost as nice as his blue suit jacket and burgundy silk tie.

"Dorian said you're looking for a new job." The subtle English accent was not so subtle in the Dallas bar, no matter how high end the furnishings or atmosphere. "Had a bit of a hot spot somewheres?"

Renner eyed Dorian, who sat across from him in a plush cushioned chair. The reason for this introduction to his boss. At least they had a table in the corner, away from other guests this time. Not in the middle of a breakfast diner for all the world to hear.

Dorian only sipped on his bourbon.

"I take it he didn't tell you the whole story." He shifted in his chair. His jeans and buttoned shirt felt too casual for a place like this. Especially with both men in front of him in a suit and tie.

Duane shook his head. "No. I don't need to hear it either, unless your former hot spot could carry over to cause problems for my business."

He shook his head. *Nope, everyone's dead.*

"I can say with full confidence you'd fit right in. I have a huge customer base that goes nutty for military men. A feature that's not currently represented in my agency."

"What customer base is that, exactly?"

The man studied him with a small smile. "You're skeptical. I understand. But keep in mind I don't hire just anyone. You need to audition first. If you're expecting free dates, a steady flow of income, and a good time in the sack with a bunch of different women, no matter what reason you have, then this role isn't for you."

Renner tapped his foot under the table. "Isn't this illegal?"

Duane scoffed, and sipped a sparkling water. "My business is one hundred percent legitimate. I will make this perfectly clear. Sex for money is illegal. But that's not what we sell. In a traditional escort agency, clients pay for an escort's time, for so-called arm candy. Whatever the client and the escort decide to do on their date is *their* business. But my clients aren't hiring any mere escort. They hire Knights."

"What's the difference?"

The manager smiled, the kind that most women would consider dashing, but Renner only expected him to sell him something. "I'm glad you asked. A handsome mug and being gifted in the sack doesn't cut it. Knights focus on the client's value. Not just for what they pay, but what they need. We cater to their hearts and minds, and make them feel valued, not just for their bodies and pocket books."

Dorian's smile widened behind his bourbon.

As the waitress dropped off another highball, Duane handed her a credit card. When she left, he continued.

"The Knights of Texas Agency employs Knights for high-end cliental. They expect a strict higher standard, as do I. So, I provide a higher title than an escort. Hence, Knights."

"Quite fitting, for the owner who is clearly from England."

He shrugged with a not-so-humble grin. "Here in the States, I can get away with it."

Renner crossed his arms and absorbed Duane's words. The man knew how to sell himself, *and* his business. He clearly had a taste for finer things, and carried himself in the same manner. Semantics made it legal, but could he really see himself in this job?

"Look." Duane leaned forward and rested his elbows on the table. "We'll give it a trial run. If after the first week you find you enjoy it, and if I think you're up to snuff, you'll earn your links."

"My what?"

"These," Dorian replied for his boss. He lifted his sleeve and showed the black stone cufflinks, with a diamond chip off-centered. "Any formal dates, we're required to wear them."

"Among a few other rules specific to Knights, and with a few additional perks, it's a simple job." Duane signed the credit card slip with which the waitress returned. "But, simple does not mean easy."

"You ready to make a shit-ton of money?" Dorian grinned.

Chapter
TWO

RENNER

The fiftieth date as a Knight, and Renner still felt jittery walking up a client's walkway. Not that he'd ever let it show. No, on the outside he was confident, collected, charming and savvy. Those were the job requirements. An easy transition from personal protection services.

He still made clients feel safe and secure with no judgments.

Only now he carried a different kind of gun.

The neighborhood was quiet. Only a few chirping crickets and a breeze rustling the towering oak trees. And his footsteps echoing on the pavestone walkway. Suburbia heaven ought to be this quiet at eleven o'clock. The house windows were dark, the entire residence seemed shut down, except for a single spotlight by the front door.

This woman was definitely new to the high-end Knight business.

The only other thing Duane had told him was her request for an overnight engagement—no formal wear required. Yet he still wore his black stone cufflinks, the signifier of an official Knight.

He glanced across the perfectly manicured lawn, to the minivan parked in the driveway. Had to be a divorcee.

Divorcees were usually the kinkiest patrons. Creative and passionate, most likely from years of having those qualities squashed in a dead marriage.

Renner had several divorcees as regulars. All part of the Knight territory.

This brand new client would certainly be interesting.

He swallowed his breath mint, and rang the doorbell.

Images flashed in his mind of his previous divorcee customer. Always dressed in their most form fitting outfits, deep cleavages and high heels, impeccable makeup no matter their age. And they were always loud under the sheets. Some, with no sheets.

Finally the door opened, and Renner put on his best smile. The one meant to make women smolder. The perfect match with his dark jeans and Armani shirt and vest.

The woman wore cotton pajamas, faded green-checkered pants, with her honey-blonde hair pulled into a loose ponytail. At first glance, she didn't have on a smudge of makeup. In fact, she almost looked beaten to a pulp with the dark circles under her eyes.

She was young. Too young to be married, let alone a

divorcee.

Do I have the wrong house?

Everything about her looked soft. Her cheekbones, her chin line, and neck. And those eyes—the deepest green tropical jungles would envy.

"You're from the agency?" she asked, a tiny smile barely breaking her thin lips.

"Yes." He cleared his throat. "I'm Renner. Pleased to meet you."

"Cassie. Please come in."

When she stepped back, he noticed her bare feet. No toenail polish. But they were small and adorable, much like the rest of her. Despite the *Walking Dead* look on her face.

The fact she didn't reach to shake his hand bothered him.

Cassie was going to play it shy. Definitely a newbie. But Renner would accommodate her. Anything to make her feel safe and secure.

Shoving his hands in his pockets, he stepped inside.

Everything screamed housewife. This was the house of married life. Clean, but cluttered. Homey furniture with couches shoved against walls and a well-used coffee table. A layout of convenience. Pictures of a little boy scattered everywhere. A stack of mail sat a foot high on the dining room table.

Not the normal client.

"Thanks for coming on short notice." She stepped around him, careful not to brush him when she walked past.

She's nervous. Renner couldn't help but smile.

"Can I get you something to drink? Soda, beer, wine?"

"Whatever you're having." His standard reply, whenever a client didn't specify.

"I don't drink," Cassie replied quickly. "But I have a beer if you'd like."

"Sure, thanks."

He made sure not to touch anything as he followed her to the kitchen, at a distance. Clearly his presence unnerved her—odd—and he didn't want to invade her personal space. Not yet. Not that the place made him uncomfortable, though the toddler toys piled in the corner of the kitchen was a new one.

Crap, there's a kid in the house?

"Not your normal cliental, am I?"

Dead right. Renner merely smiled and took the beer. Their hands grazed each other, and he could've sworn her fingers were as icy as the can.

She crossed her arms under her small breasts. No bra, either.

Several empty boxes of muffin mix littered the counter, and a sink full of used bowls and muffin tins. A huge platter of muffins piled high filled the room with the delicious scent of blueberries and vanilla.

"My son is with my parents tonight."

"How old is he?"

"Five," she replied on a sigh and moved away.

Something didn't add up. Why hire a Knight and be confident enough to bring them to your house, and then act standoffish? Almost scared. Renner didn't push the clients. They always revealed what they wanted in the end. He'd be patient. Supportive, no matter how long it took. After all, she'd paid for the whole night.

"How long have you been in the escort business?" Cassie sat in the only armchair in the living room, leaving the entire couch to him.

Definitely not open to being touched yet.

"I've been a Knight for about six months."

She tilted her head. "Is that different than a regular escort?"

"Higher end. Focus on more than just physical."

She tightened her hold on her arms, and nodded.

"I was in personal protection for several years before that."

"Like a bodyguard?"

"Mm-hm." He took a sip of beer and reclined on the couch, trying to reassure her with his own calm behavior. Anything to get this woman to relax. She was stiffer than a two-by-four.

"What kind of people did you guard?"

"Executives, the occasional stalker victim, and a few entertainment professionals."

"And what, the escort business pays better?"

The hint of condescension in her voice didn't throw him.

However, he wasn't breaking any ice on this woman, which would definitely make for a difficult night. Renner needed to find out her motives. "They pay about the same, but Knights have a little less danger involved."

She nodded, then yawned. An actual yawn.

That threw him. But what threw him more was the glint of a gold band on her left ring finger as she covered her mouth.

Not a divorcee. Or if she was, it wasn't her choice.

"So tell me, Cassie, why did you call the agency?"

A desperate look crossed her face and erased just as quickly. She swallowed and shifted into business mode.

Like what she was about to ask was extremely hard but refused to be judged for it.

"I need some help."

That much was clear. "How can I help?"

"To be honest, I'd like to go upstairs now."

Wow. Direct. I can handle that.

Renner set his beer on the coffee table and stood. He'd definitely go upstairs with this woman. She looked like she had a mountain of problems and needed a good tussle in the sheets. He was good at that. He held out his hand and waited for her to take it.

Looking down at her made her small frame look tiny and vulnerable. As if something had beat Cassie into a ragged doll. The potential for Jessica Rabbit was extreme.

Taking his hand, she stood, and her tired eyes stared into his for several seconds.

When Renner stepped toward her, she tugged her hand away and retreated to the stairs.

Not sure what game she's playing, but I'll help as best I can.

He followed, noticing the closed doors throughout the upper floor. The wood floors were scratched and dented, no doubt from hours of toddler toys and playtime. Very lived-in.

Her bedroom was the only open door. Also very lived-in. Queen-sized bed with a rose flowered bedspread, cushy carpet and a reading nook by the window. At least twenty books piled on the nightstand and a box of tissues. Definitely her side of the bed.

The rest of the room was tidy. Too tidy.

Not a single candle, no music playing, nothing romantic about this setting. The nightstand on the other side of the bed was empty. What caught his eyes the most were the small holes in every wall. All the picture frames had been removed.

"The bathroom is in here," Cassie pushed on, ignoring his perusal. "I've put out fresh towels for you if you'd like a shower." She showed him around the attached master bath as if he were staying in a hotel or sleeping over at his mother's house.

Definitely a divorcee. Not a single photo of an ex-husband anywhere.

"Cassie." He stopped her and tried to catch her hand, but she moved away.

She was beautiful. In a reserved, scared squirrel way. If

only she'd let her guard down. For a rather stoic lady, she fidgeted a lot.

"I'll help you relax," he promised with a gentle smile. "It's what I do best."

"I didn't hire you for sex," she rushed, and hugged herself, as if the thought made her sick.

"Of course not. That's illegal." Renner smiled. "You hired my companionship. My time. I'm all yours, for the entire night." He moved to her again, wanting to wrap his arms around her and start her night of stress-relief, but she stepped out of his reach.

"I'll be right back." She escaped to the bathroom and shut the door.

He took in a raspy breath. He still hadn't discovered what she wanted. Any time he went to touch her, she scooted away like he had leprosy. The first client who didn't seem attracted to him. It crawled up his skin like the scorpions in the Afghan desert.

Not every woman was into the tall, muscular, crew-cut soldier. He hadn't met any of those before. Not that he should take it personally. Cassie hadn't given his agency any preferences for the kind of Knight she wanted, and sometimes clients changed their minds.

Rationalizing her behavior didn't make him feel better. Damn, this was just like his first appointment. A freshman pledge in a big man's game, blowing his payoff too early.

Cassie needed help with something. That much was

obvious. It was his *job* to help.

While she finished in the bathroom, he slipped off his shoes and took off his vest, draping it over the empty nightstand.

As his cufflinks and shirt followed, she appeared with her hair draped over her shoulders. Long and wavy, with a crease where her hair band had been. Fresh, casual, almost a beach style with slender curves in all the right grooves.

Bare-chested, he stood before her and watched her reaction.

"What are you doing?" she asked, eyes wide.

"What do you think?" He smirked.

Her mouth bobbed and she stared at his chest, her eyes visibly dropping down his abs and to his pants, then up to his face again. Pure shock. He smiled.

"That's not what I meant."

Renner sat on the bed and crossed his arms. "I thought this is what you wanted, Cassie. You paid a higher rate for the entire night at your private residence. The first thing you want to do is come straight upstairs. My assumption was intimacy. I apologize if I guessed wrong."

The desperate frown on her angelic face tugged at his heart.

Something's wrong.

"Renner, I just want you to sleep with me."

He gave a nervous chuckle. "Agreed. Shall we?"

Cassie sighed. "I mean, sleep beside me. Nothing

physical."

That's a curve ball. "You just want me to *sleep* next to you?"

"I know it's an awkward request for someone in your profession, but...I just want you to lay on this side of the bed, and stay there all night while I sleep."

He drew a blank. Who paid that much money just for sleep? "I'll do whatever you want, Cassie."

"Thank you," she sighed. The relief on her face rippled to the muscles in her shoulders.

"Divorce?"

She gave him a resigned stare. Her voice cracked when she spoke. "You can do whatever you like. Watch TV, read a book, sleep, anything. Just...don't leave the bed until I wake up."

If Cassie didn't look so exhausted, he might've pressed for more info. She'd skirted the question well.

She walked around the bed and literally climbed in from three feet off the floor. Cassie ruffled the pillow and tucked her tiny feet in the sheets while Renner lay on his side, crossing his ankles.

"Would you like another pillow?" she asked as she handed him the remote.

"I'm good, Cass."

He might as well have sworn in a silent church, because everything in the room stopped.

"Don't call me that." Her face turned blank, almost

ghostlike.

Ah, button number one. "All right. Cassie it is."

The pale green tank top hugged her figure perfectly and the fresh soap smell wafted from her smooth skin. While it wasn't the typical nightwear his clients wore for bed, she was certainly seductive in her cute, college girl way. She didn't look much older than that, either.

She reached over her head and turned off the lamp, then snuggled into her pillow. "Good night, Renner. And thank you."

The way she'd whispered his name and thanked him with her eyes closed, set his protective instincts into hyper-mode.

This woman paid to have a stranger sleep next to her in her own bed. No doubt she could use a good night's sleep as much as phenomenal sex. Maybe the most helpful thing in the world to this sweet creature was something simpler.

He slowly closed the two-foot gap between them and wrapped his arm around her middle, spooning her body with the gentle touch of a full body hug.

Cassie's head shot up instantly. "What're you doing?"

"Helping you relax," he cooed in her ear.

"Please don't. I just...need to sleep." The desperation in her voice almost sounded like crying. "I haven't really slept in a long time."

It took all his military training to hide his bruised ego.

What else can I do to get this woman to give?

"Go ahead." Renner struggled to use his most soothing voice. "I promise I won't try to kiss you or seduce you, unless you ask me to. Just relax and try to sleep."

Her whole body had gone back to a stiff board and she pulled away. Flipping on the light, she sat up and looked at him, as if studying a stranger in the middle of a street. "I appreciate trying to help me relax, Renner. But...I don't want this."

"Okay." There was only one avenue left. Brutal honesty. "You just looked like you really could use a hug. No expectations, nothing intimate, Cassie. I promise."

They sat beside each other in silence.

Renner watched her fatigued and tortured expression bounce between him and her side of the bed. He hated feeling useless. Like his presence was the exact opposite of what she wanted.

I guess I'm not as good at protecting as I thought.

It was several minutes before she spoke again. "You're wearing his cologne."

He almost didn't hear her, she was so quiet, but he swore he could hear her heart cracking.

This was not a divorcee, no matter what his boss had assumed. This was much worse. And it was his presence that made her act this way. More specifically, his scent.

"I'll wash it off," he whispered, and moved to climb out of the bed. But she held his arm with the grip of a drowning victim.

"Don't."

Neither of them moved.

He sat there, letting her cling to his arm until she settled. A war of emotions battled across her pretty face. Renner wanted desperately to create peace, at least a truce and ease her pain. Everything he'd done up to this point had only driven her further away.

Asking who 'he' was would make it worse, given Cassie's fortified shyness. Although he was certain *who* shared the same cologne. The same man who was in all the missing frames. The man who'd put that ring on her finger.

Was this a military man? Had she been visited by that black car with a chaplain, no doubt with her son playing in the house? Too many of his friends' wives had been visited by two Marines with news worse than anyone should ever have to bear. She'd probably given them the same anguished look that she gave him now.

"Do you want a hug, Cassie?"

Her emerald eyes watered as she studied him, and he worried she'd refuse. Finally, she nodded.

Renner opened his arms and let her rest her head on his shoulder. Her arms tightened around him as he heard her breathe in his scent.

Another man's cologne.

For several long minutes, her breathing was uneven and often came in tiny gasps. Like she was fighting tears.

Her hair smelled of raspberry shampoo and Irish Spring

soap. The amber light from the lamp cast a cinnamon sheen across her blonde locks. Everything about this woman almost broke his reserve. The raw emotions pouring out of her were a weapon of love that no battalion could thwart.

Hunkering down into the pillows and covers, he wrapped her in his arms and felt her muscles slowly give. Gradually, her breathing evened and the firm grip around his back loosened.

It didn't matter how long she slept or that he still wore jeans. Or that she drifted off to sleep thinking of another man. After only a few minutes, Cassie was deep asleep on his shoulder, and Renner just watched the rhythmic rise and fall of her back. Wet drops landed on his shoulder.

Careful not to wake her, he shifted just enough to see a few tears drift down her cheek. "Cassie?" he whispered. He'd seen a lot as a bodyguard and a Knight, and even more as a soldier. But he couldn't handle a woman crying. From her even breathing, she was asleep.

His arms squeezed tighter, gentle and reassuring, and her whole body sighed against him.

Cassie needed more than just a good night's sleep. Suddenly, this night was more than just another job or another client.

More than making someone feel safe or wanted. This was a desperate honor, a privilege to be here for Cassie during a dark moment. Perhaps, her darkest. Eventually, he slipped off and they both slept in the dim glow of the lamp.

CASSIE

A few cracks of early light spanned across Cassie's face and she opened her eyes. A dark sunrise peeked through the blinds, but the brightness of the room confused her. Ah, the lamp was still on.

Something moved beneath her. *Not a pillow.*

Suddenly the world rushed back into her brain, and she remembered.

Renner...the escort.

Wearing that cologne and looking just like...

He'd stayed with her. The entire night.

I slept the entire night?

The clock on her nightstand glowed blue. *6:55 a.m.*

Thank God. Relief flooded her body and she hugged the strange, yet welcome form beside her. All she knew was his name, that he used to be a bodyguard, and had the same affinity for colognes. This man had given her the one thing she really needed. The first straight night's sleep in six months.

It didn't matter that she'd had to pay for it.

"Good morning, Cassie," the man's sultry voice cooed.

She sat up and looked at him, watching his too-good-to-be-real smile and hazel eyes glowing into hers. Bare chiseled chest, light tan and defined abs filled her bed. Cassie could see why a woman would fall for this escort, but she knew better.

Her heart wouldn't let her connect after what she'd been through. Especially, not with an *escort*. Nevertheless, she was grateful he'd stayed with her, no expectations or assumptions.

No judgments, either.

"You slept well," Renner continued when she didn't say anything.

"Thanks to you," she sighed and brushed her hair back, not really caring that it was a crazy mess.

Light shadows lined his eyes, and a hint of stubble covered his chin. He pulled off the sleepy warrior look to perfection.

"Did you sleep at all?"

With a noncommittal shrug, he yawned. "A bit. I enjoyed the company."

Cassie smiled, but pulled away. The whole exchange felt entirely too intimate. Slipping off the bed, the carpet felt cold to her bare feet. She escaped to the bathroom and did her business. When she returned, he'd already stood and redressed. The chic and trendy vest and jeans combination looked good on him.

What amazed her more was that she actually paid attention. The last six months had been on autopilot, making it one hour to the next, let alone day-to-day. Keeping her son on as normal schedule as possible kept her moving, despite moments of emotional chaos. Those weak moments were easier to handle at home. Public breakdowns were luxuries she couldn't afford. Not with Landon.

Hiring Renner was the last thing she'd ever expected to do. Desperation had driven her to it. How could she possibly explain to her family and friends?

Standing before him, Cassie could still smell a hint of the cologne that had made her drift to sleep.

He took her hands, cupping them in both of his and kissed her knuckles. His calluses were rough and easily defined.

"I can't believe you stayed," she mumbled.

"You asked me to." Renner quirked a confused smile at her. "It's what you needed."

It's what I paid for.

She couldn't stop the thought from jumping in. The purpose of escorts—their stereotype—wasn't lost on her. Not that she'd ever indulge. Cassie hadn't been brought up that way. It wasn't the kind of home she'd created for Landon.

"Cassie, not that I'm not happy to be here and give you what you wanted, but why did you call the agency for this? Just a warm body in the bed, couldn't a friend have done this?"

The question was inevitable. Although, he'd gone the entire night before he'd asked. Or maybe she was just that tired; he hadn't gotten to it before she'd collapsed.

"I didn't want someone I knew. Who knew me, and what...happened. The constant questions or talking about it, or the...pity. I didn't want another reminder."

When he opened his mouth to push for more, she rushed the rest.

"Asking this of another man who may have wanted to take it further was out of the question. I don't want any hassles or entanglements with personal feelings or intimacy." A crushing pain gripped her abdomen, the same she always felt when her mind wandered to *him*.

Or the thought of asking for help. That was just as worse.

"Can I ask what happened?"

Her airways squeezed shut. *Not this, please. Not after my first night of real sleep.*

"It's okay," Renner amended, clearly reading what had to be anguish on her face.

Something in his eyes caught her attention. Something that told her he cared, and his protective nature was hurt by her refusal.

"I'd rather just be alone. I have a lot to do today." The mail was the first she swore to get through. It screamed at her every time she walked by.

Renner sighed and kissed her knuckles again. "It was lovely to meet you, Cassie. If you need anything else, just call." He reached into his pocket and pulled out a card. His name and phone number were etched in white letters across a pewter background. Nothing else. "For discretion." His smile was more genuine than before.

"Thank you, Renner," she replied. She read his last name off the card. "Renner Shaw."

"Anytime."

Cassie kept her feet planted to the carpet as he clopped down the stairs.

He'd been exactly what she'd needed. An understanding person with no attachments or preconceptions about her. To fill a space so she could recoup and build energy. Today would be the first in her life that she was truly alone.

No Landon. No Kyle...

Did she want to go to bed that way tonight? If she could sleep at all.

What if all that would happen was her tossing and crying all night in a truly empty house? Merely only a reflection of her heart.

Alone, broken and empty.

"Renner?" She managed to keep from sounding panicked, and ran out of her bedroom.

He stood by the open door with his hand on the knob. He smiled up at her as she gripped the railing.

"Are you free tonight?"

His smile slipped.

Oh God. He thinks I'm asking him out. How many customers had he turned down?

"Um..." He rubbed the back of his neck.

"I'm just hoping for another night's sleep, is all. And if you're not booked..."

The poignant stare he gave her made her stop. "I'll be here, Cassie."

Chapter
THREE

RENNER

Another overnight appointment, prepaid, on Renner's calendar. At least expectations weren't a mystery. This felt different. Not like he was a Knight, but in his bodyguard role. Just a different kind of guarding.

His forte; he'd loved it. The job requirements had fit his protective nature perfectly. He'd been that way since he was a kid. But too many close calls, including that last critical trip to the hospital, had forced him to change careers.

Renner strode up Cassie's walkway in jeans and a gray t-shirt, carrying a bag of goodies for the night. Not the typical chocolates and flowers for a date, or even 'toys' for some of his eccentric clients.

These were just for Cassie. To make her smile, and more importantly, relax.

When he rang the doorbell, her voice drifted through.

"It's open."

The house was picked up, complete with vacuum streaks on the carpeting. Lemon cleaner filled the air, and Cassie stood by the sink with her back turned.

She was in her comfortable pajamas again, and cute bare feet. Good. Just what he'd hoped for. Her hair was loose this time, falling just below her shoulder blades.

"I brought a few surprises for you." He grinned and set the bag on the kitchen table. The stack of mail had now been reduced to a small pile of papers. No blueberry muffin mix boxes on the counter, and the sink was empty. She'd been busy.

Cassie turned and spotted the bag, a confused smile on her lips.

Words dissipated. *This* was a different woman in front of him. Nothing zombie about her.

Pink cheeks, smooth hair framing her unwrinkled face combined with smiling eyes. Revived and...comfortable.

Beautiful.

"What?" she asked.

"You look great."

A grin split her face. "No, what's in the bag?"

"Oh. Yeah..." *Smooth move, jackoff.* Renner pulled out several bags of popcorn and three movies. "First surprise. Your pick between two action flicks or a comedy. Time to check our brains at the door for the night." He'd been careful not to pick romances or dramas. She'd clearly experienced enough of both recently.

Cassie really had an excellent smile with perfectly straight teeth. The kind people paid thousands for orthodontists to copy. Totally understandable how a guy could fall in love with her at first grin.

Not that that was what this was.

"Fantastic choices, Renner." She picked the comedy and grabbed the popcorn. "You get that started and I'll heat these up."

Goal number one, get her to smile— accomplished.

"What's the other surprise?" she called from the kitchen as he fiddled with the machine.

"That's for later," he grinned.

For goal number two.

When Cassie chose the opposite side of the couch than Renner, each with their own little bowl of popcorn, a twinge of disappointment panged his chest. She still didn't trust him. Or care for any show of intimacy. However, the fact that she hadn't chosen the armchair on the other side of the room was promising. Loosening up a little at a time.

He couldn't expect overnight transformations. Particularly with something this dramatic in her life. It wasn't like Renner could ease her worries with a quick romp, or even a heart stopping make-out session.

Many clients expected dripping heat the second he pressed the doorbell, to escape their lives even for an hour. That was his goal for every one of them. To help them escape.

Not with Cassie.

Digging to his roots—his protective instincts—was the only thing that would help her.

Although, he'd stop at calling himself a savior. He'd been careful in this new career to distance himself from that label. It had too much responsibility, coupled with unachievable expectations. Like that damn magazine declaring the Sexiest Man Alive had any implications on bedroom skills.

Renner's were exceptional, of course.

"What are you smirking at?" Cassie broke into his thoughts.

"Um…just glad to see you relaxed," he half-lied. "You've clearly had a busy day."

"Oh, yeah. All that just…snuck up on me. But it's easier to get all of it done without my son running around the house."

"Does your mom have him again tonight?"

"Actually…" She fiddled with a popcorn kernel between her fingers. "My mom and dad took him camping for the week. Get him away from everything so I could…sleep." Her smile slowly disappeared as she spoke. Cassie's eyes were on one of the kid's pictures on the shelf of knick-knacks across the room.

The love and worry in her eyes reminded him of several clients he'd protected as a bodyguard. Mothers were the ultimate figures in that role. Guarding not only their children's bodies, but their minds and hearts as well.

An endless job, from which no one ever retired. And

never grew easier with time.

Now, she had to do it alone. With no one to protect her.

"You think too much," she broke in again.

Renner chuckled. "That's my line."

Throughout the movie, he let her slowly relax on the couch without impeding on her space. She'd chuckled in a few places, but no outright laughter. Maybe she'd seen the movie before, but that didn't matter. Her small smile had been in place for most of the flick. Toward the end, Renner noticed her legs weren't curled as tightly underneath her, and her toes were only a few inches away from his thigh.

Time for goal number two.

Renner pushed himself off the couch and grabbed the bag from the table.

"Where are you going?"

"Just keep watching. I'll be right back."

Chapter FOUR

CASSIE

Cassie had seen the movie before, but it didn't matter. Renner had clearly shown he cared about helping her. Warmth spread through her torso. She had to admit his genuine smile and eagerness were a bit contagious. His preference of movies was noteworthy.

Even after he'd left the room, his cologne lingered in the air. Not the same scent he'd worn last night. Probably a smart thing. This one was more woodsy and earthy. He had good taste there, as well.

Everything about him was in good taste—clothes, manners, general grooming.

Except his profession.

Who went from a bodyguard to an escort?

A faint rushing noise whooshed overhead. The water pipes.

He's taking a bath?

Cassie went to the stairs, but when her hand reached the railing, she stopped.

Trusting people was difficult, at least right now. So much of her life was in chaos and it was hard to let go of the little control she held. This was her house and it was the easiest thing to claim power over.

But she'd told him to feel free to use the bathroom. TV, music, anything.

It's just a freakin' bath, Cass. Get over it.

She returned to the couch and curled her feet under her legs. It was a decent summer night outside, but shivers rippled through her body, and the chenille blanket didn't cut it. What chilled her more was anticipating what normally came after the shivers.

Panic attacks.

It'd happened every night since...

Cassie had never had one until that first day back from the hospital. She'd been alone, would never be held by him again, never hear the garage door open when he returned from work. Would never kiss him again. Their plans for another child were dashed. Landon would always be an only child.

Her heart caved and she squeezed her legs to her chest, making herself as small as possible. Everything closed in on her and all she could see was her knees, trembling at the end of the tunnel. A vise gripped her lungs and breathing was impossible.

No, Cassie. The therapist's voice broke through in some distant void. *Open up. You can't breathe if you're all closed. Open everything.*

She forced her legs to the floor and pressed into the couch.

Open the body, open your fists, even your mouth. Get as wide as you can.

One deep breath after another, the tunnel vision slowly subsided and tingles raced through her limbs.

Her therapist had suggested anti-anxiety meds or anti-depressants, whatever she thought would help. A drug addict's dream sat right in front of her, her choice of prized pills, and she flat out rejected them.

Her body had never responded well to over-the-counter medication, so Lord knew what kind of damage those prescription suckers would inflict on her already-frail body. She needed a good night's sleep, not a coma-inducer.

"Cassie?"

She opened her eyes and saw him, upside down, leaning against the railing.

Everything stopped.

Sparkling blue eyes, wavy blond hair, and that incredible, smiling stare that'd made her heart melt the first time they met. And every moment since. It couldn't be...

Whirling around, she focused again. Kyle's image was gone. Instead, the form that gripped the railing was Renner. There was no mistaking the hazel eyes and short dark hair.

Inquisitive stare.

Great, now I'm hallucinating. Maybe I do need those meds.

"What're you doing?" he asked.

"Just...laying here." Caught, spread open like a bug on a windshield. Cassie cringed and wanted to crawl under the couch.

"Well, if you're done with the movie." He nodded to the TV, where the credits scrolled through. "Surprise number two is ready for you."

She took another deep breath and pushed off the couch. The tingling had settled and walking wasn't difficult. She probably looked as winded as she felt.

When she reached the railing, Renner took her hand and helped her up the stairs. His palm was warm and the callused fingers proved him a man of action, hard work, and little down time. Her clammy hand felt tiny in his.

"You're all wound up again," he commented in a soothing voice. "Relax."

"I'm fine." Her tight response failed at sounding calm.

"It's all right." He squeezed her hand. "I have something to help with that."

Oh God. Please don't let this be another attempt at...his job.

Her escort guided her to the bedroom, where she sighed in relief. Exactly as it was before. But...he kept walking. When he opened the bathroom door, she stopped.

Renner had run a bath. With lavender scented bubbles, tealight candles scattered throughout the room, and a mini-loofah sitting on the ledge. The mirror was fogged over and gentle music flowed from his phone tucked away on the counter.

The thought and effort he'd put behind this touched her, just as the warmth in the humid bathroom eased the shivers from before. The lavender was heavenly, but Cassie couldn't remember buying that scent. He must've brought it with him, along with all the candles.

Wait. Does he intend to...

"This is just for you," he broke in, as if he'd read her mind. "So you can wipe the scared rabbit look from your face."

"You did all this for me?"

"I got you to smile. Now, my goal is to get you to relax. In private."

Not likely, after a semi-panic attack.

"Take your time. Come down when you're ready."

With a squeeze of her shoulder, Renner closed the door behind him.

She stood by the tub and let the humid air soak her face. Heat absorbed through her clothes and ebbed the remaining tremors. Cassie hadn't had a bath in years. Showers were faster, more efficient and easier to clean.

The music switched to a soothing piano melody...Yanni, from the sound of it.

Renner knew how to please a woman. Kind of a job

requirement. Whether skills he learned on the job, or a natural ability, she couldn't guess. As sweet as he was, he was still a stranger. A kind and thoughtful stranger. She didn't trust him yet. With his penchant for jumping straight to intimacy from the previous night, it was likely she couldn't. *What else should I expect?* It was a possibility from the moment she picked up the phone to order his services.

Cassie turned the lock. Then peeled off her clothes and tested the water. Nice and hot, but not scalding.

Entering a bathtub wasn't like peeling off a bandage. To truly savor it, submerging needed to be slow. "Screw it," she murmured and dunked herself completely.

The water burned her face, but she liked it. It was the fastest way to chase away the remnants of her panic attack. No sound, no demands, no pressures from the outside. Just the swirling heat encasing her like a womb.

Taking her time, Cassie scrubbed every inch and absorbed the lavender like a drug. If she drank, this would be a perfect time for a glass of wine. Or a bottle. The relaxing music would have to be enough.

Time escaped and she lost track of how many songs changed. When the water turned lukewarm and her skin pruned, she climbed out and let the bubbles cascade down her legs. She'd forgotten to grab a towel from the linen closet, but her Turkish robe hung in the master closet.

A birthday gift from her husband.

She wrapped herself in it and hugged her arms for

another indiscriminate length of minutes.

Blowing out the candles filled the bathroom with the twirling smoke of burnt wicks. The scent was almost as good as the lavender.

Cassie brushed through her hair and rubbed lotion on her face. Her skin was still red from the hot bath, but that didn't matter. Renner would never see it.

Tucking herself into the robe, she unlocked the door and strode out of the bathroom. The wood floor in the hallway was cold under her bare feet, and there were no sounds coming from downstairs.

Where's Renner?

When she turned the corner, she froze. Everything the relaxing bath had done to her muscles erased as she coiled inside.

Renner stood by her son's room, peering inside the open door.

Chapter
FIVE

RENNER

All he wanted to find was a towel for Cassie. The careful planning in hopes to get her to relax, and he forgot the freakin' towel. When he opened this door, his gut dropped to his heels.

Her son's room was messy, like a little boy's room should be, but every inch was covered with pictures of what he assumed was her husband. On the night stand and dresser, snuggled between stuffed animals and hung all over the walls. The same ocean-colored eyes and lopsided smile as the kid.

So this explains where all those missing frames went.

He was too shocked to acknowledge his heart splitting.

"What are you doing?" The tiny and terrified voice behind him pulled him from the trance. Cassie stood in the hallway, bundled up in a white robe like an Eskimo, clutching the fabric with pale knuckles. Fear had glazed over her eyes faster than a fifty-foot drop could have achieved.

"I was looking for a towel."

"Shut the door," she hissed.

"Cassie—"

"Shut it."

The door-click echoed down the silent hallway.

"I wasn't snooping—" Renner watched as her cheeks changed from a blushed pink to ash in a few blinks.

Suddenly, her chest seemed to cave and she reached for her throat. Ashen cheeks turned a pallid blue before a gasp and choke escaped her colorless lips.

"Cassie?"

He'd barely moved two steps toward her before she collapsed to her knees.

She put her hands out to catch herself, but they slid off the wall like broken strings, and she fell face first. He shot forward and caught her head before it smashed into the wood planks. Her momentum rolled her sideways into his outstretched arm and she looked up at him with dilated eyes.

Panic attack.

Renner had seen his fair share as a bodyguard. Her eyes were glued to his face, but she couldn't see him. She couldn't see anything. Her hands were clenched, and her jaw was wired shut.

Scooping her rigid body into his arms, he rushed her to the bed. She hardly weighed anything, like a plywood board—light and stiff.

Her body barely sank into the mattress when he laid her down. Her knees curled up, and the hem of her robe fell open, revealing the reddened skin of her thigh up to her buttocks. Soft, almost creamy, and his breath caught. When he pulled away, his shirt was clasped between her locked fingers and he couldn't pry them open. Not without breaking them.

He unfolded himself out of his shirt, hearing a small tear in the process. More skin peeked out through her slipping robe, from her slender waist up to the valley between her breasts. Including half a dusky nipple. Goosebumps rose all over the revealed skin. His eyes traced down her trembling body.

Renner recovered her with the robe and began opening up her body. The trick was to open everything—except the robe—while using his voice to soothe away the panic. "Open up, Cassie."

He pushed her legs down and pulled her arms to the side. Slowly, he kneaded her fingers to release and spread out her palms. Then he moved to her face and gently massaged her jaw, just under her ears. What should've been rubbing a pillow, soft and agile, was nothing less than a concrete block.

"Open, Cassie. Breathe."

Gradually, her mouth parted and he felt her first deep breath under his arm. Her pupils narrowed and the muted emerald of her irises acknowledged him.

"There you are."

Her breathing grew deeper with each second. As Renner's anxiety ebbed along with hers, he noticed the lavender scent all over her skin. Mixed with her own unique fragrance, the sweet combination and the vision of her bare body plagued his senses.

"So much for the relaxing bath," he muttered.

"Renner," she panted.

God, her voice is so enticing, pleading.

Their lips were a candle-flame apart.

"Yes, Cassie?"

"Can you get off me now?"

Renner set the highball glass in front of Cassie.

She grimaced. "I don't want to drink that."

His client was still pale. Not as white as her robe, but at least she'd stopped gasping for air to control her anxiety. Tonight had been a failure. She was just as coiled as last night.

Only now, Renner was just as tight. He'd never take advantage of a woman, especially in that state. Whether she knew it or not, Cassie was a damn knockout. And thoroughly irresistible.

"It'll calm you faster than a bath," he urged, pouring a glass of whiskey for himself. "Though not as fast as a Xanax."

"Are you trying to get me hooked on alcohol to solve my anxiety problems?"

"One drink does not make you an alcoholic."

She eyeballed the glass again, the scowl more defined.

"Just one sip, and then wait five minutes." Renner

plopped in the chair across from her and put the glass to his lips. Finding the untouched bottle of whiskey in the cabinet above the fridge was nothing less than a miracle. There were only two choices; this or tequila. A newbie like Cassie would find the tequila too abrasive.

"Hardly feels like the right circumstances to start the habit."

He chuckled. "You don't know the real purpose behind a good drink."

She pursed her lips and held the glass between her fingers. Staring at it like a vial of rancid medicine, Cassie took a deep breath and forced a gulp of the amber liquid.

The gulp rippled down her delicate neck to the hollow base of her throat; adorable and just as creamy as the rest of her skin. It warmed him more than the whiskey and settled in his gut.

He shifted in his chair and took another sip.

God, Renner. She's just a client.

"That's strong," Cassie choked between a cough and a wince.

"The choices were limited. Sorry."

"I forgot he had these up there."

He watched her, refusing to respond to the last comment. Mentioning her husband wasn't on his list of things he'd expected her to say.

For a long moment, they both sat in silence. As if she waited for him to ask a probing question just so she could ignore it. Renner wanted her to feel comfortable talking about anything. Pushing her always made her back off.

Still wet from the bath, her hair was pulled up into a clip. The darker ash hue brought out a touch of olive in her skin, as if a distant portion of her was Latina. The clover eyes reminded him of the Irish highlands depicted in travel magazines. And were just as deep.

"Do you mind putting on a shirt?" Cassie blurted.

Renner coughed through a sip. "What?"

"Your abs are...distracting."

He held back a chuckle, but not a smile. *So is your neck.* "You ripped my shirt earlier."

"I did?" She finally looked up.

"You have the grip of a ninja."

"Oh." Her cheeks flamed, but it was hard to tell whether from attraction or embarrassment. "I'm sorry."

He shrugged and took another sip.

"Thanks for...helping." She ducked her eyes again.

"I wouldn't leave you alone in the middle of that."

"I'm sure it's not the kind of thing you expected to deal with as a..."

Renner set down his glass and waited for her to finish. Couldn't help the glare. Through her scowl and cutting tone, he'd expected her to make some snide comment about escorts. Or gigolos, whatever label she wanted to slap on him.

But she didn't finish.

"I'm not a heartless prick, out for an easy score or a quick payday, Cassie."

His harsh tone caught her full attention.

She squirmed and squeezed the glass.

"When I see someone who needs help," he continued, unable to keep the edge in his voice. "I help them. Simple as that." Chalk it up to his protective nature, but he hated sounding defensive. He'd never felt the need to justify his job choice—most of the time it wasn't worth fighting. People had stereotypes locked in their brains tighter than Fort Knox. Defending it with Cassie was different. For some reason, her approval mattered.

Only God knew why.

"You sound just like him."

The words caught him off guard. Again, she didn't need to specify who *'him'* was. Her husband. Still, Renner wasn't a fan of what felt like jealousy swirling in his abdomen.

She wasn't blushing anymore and had stopped fidgeting. The alcohol must have kicked in. Her grip loosened on the glass and her shoulders weren't as bunched under the robe.

"So direct, no nonsense, and everything is black and white."

Renner hid a smile when he watched her scowl down another sip of whiskey. Pointing out his surprise at her less reserved behavior would've the opposite effect. So he sipped his drink again. "I never said everything was black and white," he prodded.

"You don't have to," Cassie returned and reclined in the

chair.

"You don't believe in gray areas?"

After a deep sigh, she took another sip. "Gray areas are like dating. Covering the flaws long enough to entice someone to become invested in a relationship until the true nature is revealed."

"You don't believe in dating?"

"I don't believe in hiding flaws. Another way of lying."

This is what Cassie looks like uninhibited. Playfully combative, with a hint of condescension. Not what he'd expected. She certainly looked more comfortable.

"Your point is, everyone's either an angel or a devil. No middle ground?"

"I didn't say gray areas don't exist. Just that they're a waste of time."

"So, let's stop wasting it." Renner set down his whiskey and watched her eyes flare. "Tell me what you want, Cassie."

Their eyes locked.

Something in her stare told him not to move. Not to push. To let the words form in her mind and make their way to her mouth, past those whiskey-covered lips.

"I want to rewind," she murmured.

He tilted his head.

"I want to go back to that night, and change my mind," Cassie continued quietly, looking straight at him, but not really seeing him. "Not send him out for chocolate shakes for us, when that truck full of drunk kids wouldn't be there. When my son doesn't need his daddy's pictures all around his room to fall asleep at night."

Moisture built in her eyes, but she didn't blink.

"When I didn't feel aged twenty years overnight. Or have to call a stranger to take his place just so I could sleep."

A teardrop traced down her cheek and plopped in her whiskey glass.

A lump formed at the base of Renner's throat. She never would've revealed this much if it weren't for the alcohol. It hadn't been his intention either. Her story wasn't unique.

People died every day from drunk drivers. Cassie herself was exceptional. A survivor with an iron will. A few misconceptions clouded among her sensibilities, but strong nonetheless.

And she still considers me a stranger. Which was *true*, but why did he feel like he'd lost something important?

Her eyes locked on his face. "Is that black and white enough for you?"

Renner cleared his throat and waited before he responded. This wasn't about him. What he wanted or what he *thought* she needed. The pain in Cassie's voice and fortified barriers around her heart weren't something he could erase in a few nights, or even make sense of. It was definitely a no-fly-zone for his job. Nothing personal, or it warranted immediate cut-off, according to his boss. He couldn't help but to reach out and try.

"Not that I'm a therapist." He swirled the last few drops

of whiskey in the glass. "But the last thing you need is to separate your feelings into neatly organized boxes in your head. Anger in a black box, happiness in a white box. Or go crazy figuring out where to shove the stuff that doesn't make sense. For lack of a better cliché, life is unfair and...messy."

"Like gray areas?"

His lip lifted in a small smile, but he shook his head. "No. Life is shit-loaded with colors, including gray."

If he'd just materialized from thin air, Cassie couldn't have looked more stunned. "That's...pretty deep." A wisp of hair, dryer than the rest, fell from her clip and dangled against her cheek.

Honey against her vanilla skin. Full of color.

"Yeah. Even deeper is to choose to see the colors, or be stuck in gray areas. And as you said, aren't gray areas a waste of time?"

"You *choose* to see the colors?"

How can I not with this masterpiece sitting in front of me? "It's a hell of a lot prettier...like you."

She smiled, for the first time in over an hour. "In the grand scheme, what box would you put yourself in?"

God, this woman could make him grin like a schoolboy after his first kiss. *Keep the smolder, Renner.* "There's no box big enough for me."

When she laughed, he lost the heat. The closest sound to angels singing, if it weren't for the tears rimming her eyes. She wiped them away. "You keep surprising me, Renner."

"Too emotionally connected?"

The combination blush and smirk she gave didn't fit the young housewife motif. More fitting for a playboy pinup in the Forbidden Fruit edition. Right in front of him, but couldn't be touched.

Cassie bit her bottom lip, which only made him inwardly groan through the torment. She lifted the glass and drank the rest of her whiskey, staring with hooded eyes over the rim of the glass.

She didn't even know she was taunting him.

"I'll admit, I judged you before you walked through that door. Before I even made the phone call to your agency. You're not what I expected."

Renner lifted an eyebrow. "You imagined a piercing-covered, thong clad debaucher?"

"Um, yeah. Without the vocabulary and emotional intelligence."

"Sorry to prove you wrong."

"I'm not."

God love her for that. "Doesn't happen often, I take it?"

A simple shake of her head deflated every ounce of confidence he possessed. He might not fit the mold she described, but it was certain how little she regarded his profession.

"I opened that door and you completely threw me. You stood there looking just like him."

He narrowed his eyes. From the pictures in the boy's

room, her husband hadn't shared a single trait with him.

"Not your hair or eyes, but the way you carried yourself." Cassie bit her lip and her eyes dropped to his mouth. "Confident and sturdy, except when you looked at me. You didn't just look me in the eyes, you saw me. Studied me like a priceless oil painting, when I know I looked like hell. That totally threw me."

"Cassie, if this is your worst, then God help me or any other man who sees you at your best."

The red that dashed her cheeks reinvigorated his pride. She really was a tidal wave on the senses, one that knocked Helen of Troy and Grace Kelly off their pedestals.

She reached across the table and touched his hand. Her skin was warm and plusher than the robe. Her eyes were even softer. "I'm glad I was wrong. Once you knew what I really wanted, you didn't judge me. You still looked at me like I mattered."

He didn't know where she was going with this, but he couldn't let her get attached. As much as her confession flattered him—hell, outright *thrilled* him—she was still a client.

Don't kid yourself, idiot. You're already attached.

He also hadn't told her about the robe falling away, but he wouldn't embarrass her further. Renner pushed his glass out of the way and flipped his palm to cover hers.

Before he could reply, she squeezed his fingers.

"Now, get rid of that panic on your face, because I'm not

confessing my love or proposing a relationship here." She smiled.

He laughed nervously, and rubbed his thumb over her knuckles. "We're just crumbling stereotypes, aren't we?"

Chapter
SIX

CASSIE

The dark room wrapped her in a secondary blanket, calming away the remnants of the panic attack. Or was that the alcohol? Her whole body was warm, on the verge of tingles, and for once she didn't feel an ache in her chest.

I can see how people get dependent.

Even Renner being beside her didn't unnerve her like last night. Although they were both under the comforter, he lay on top of the sheet, easing any doubts she had of his intentions. Which was sweet.

Staring at his bare, muscular pecs at the dining room table had been enough to get her mind wandering to places she never thought she'd think of again. Perhaps another effect of the alcohol, but now those thoughts didn't bother her. The same mass of muscles was lying beside her, prepaid on her credit card for the whole night.

What could it hurt, Cassie? There's no one to judge you,

and now you're single. One night. If he's willing, why not?

She sighed and rolled to her side.

Renner's chest slowly rose and fell under the covers and his eyes were closed. His head was slightly tilted toward her, with long lashes kissing his skin, though barely visible in the dark.

His hand was only a few inches from hers, relaxed and warm. Sleeping seemed so easy to him, and intimacy even easier.

Who better to help with her reservations than an expert?

Who are you kidding, Cass? You're not single; you're widowed. It's not about judgment. Sex was something between two people who loved each other. Not just a reason to expend energy and stress. Not to her.

This thing with Renner, it wasn't love. Respect, yes. Attraction, hell yes. She'd be a corpse not to acknowledge it. Maybe he'd become a new friend as well. But there was no hope in her for love.

They hardly knew each other. To him, this was just a business deal. What little information they'd exchanged was more about her. Renner was still a jumble of mysteries.

"It's hard to enjoy the view in the dark, Cassie."

Her gaze shot to his face, and the glassy shine in his eyes locked onto hers. His voice was low and soft, gliding along her neck in just the right way. Heat flooded her cheeks and her breath caught. "I didn't know you were awake." Her voice was airy and higher than she liked.

"I never fell asleep."

"I...was thinking."

"You were burning a hole in my forehead. Smoke is spewing from your ears."

She smiled, but she doubted he could see it. "How is this so natural to you?"

"What?"

"This...intimacy. With a different woman every time."

Cassie felt his sigh more than heard it. "You want to know why I'm in this business."

"It doesn't make sense to me," she admitted.

The sheets rustled as he moved his hand and slowly closed his fingers around hers. His palm was so warm. His thumb along her skin was hot and smooth.

Everything about him was that way.

A long time passed before he spoke again.

"The same reason you called and asked for a Knight. Not just for sleep, but...something missing you needed filled. Without complications."

"What are *you* missing?"

His thumb stopped and for a moment the whole room went silent. Even the heartbeat between her ears.

"You'll think I'm nuts."

"Then we make quite the pair." She smirked.

The sheets rustled more and his warm breath danced against her cheek. Peppermint toothpaste and sweet aftershave.

"A purpose."

The two words swirled between their breathing, soaking and absorbing the silence.

Renner rolled to his side and more of his torso faced her.

The shadows weren't as dark, now that her eyes had adjusted to the room. Now that she'd adjusted to the stranger beside her. Who suddenly wasn't so distant.

Why aren't I nervous?

"You became an escort—a Knight—to find purpose?"

"I left being a bodyguard because I lost my purpose."

"Becoming a Knight would help you find it?"

"Hardly."

"Then why do you do it?"

"To be needed," he admitted quietly. "To make someone feel safe, if only for a while."

"Wouldn't bodyguarding accomplish that?"

A grimace flashed across his face for an instant, then softened. "Not always."

"Something happened." That was easy to see, with how much he dodged questions.

His silence confirmed it.

"So you quit?"

"When you lose a client you're paid to protect, it's bad for referrals."

Renner kept swirling his fingers over her palm, gentle and feathery, as she absorbed his words. He'd lost a client.

"Oh," was all she could say.

The wrinkles in his forehead deepened as he watched her. Judging her reaction, no doubt, with understandable apprehension.

Cassie placed her hand on his chest, so warm under her fingers. His heartbeat was strong. She wanted to say, *'I'm sorry'*, but it seemed insufficient. "So, the escort thing just came to mind after?"

He shrugged and traced his finger along her arm, up to cover her hand.

It was soothing. Equally strange that it didn't bother her.

"A friend referred me after I got out of the hospital," Renner answered. "Said I had that look women would pay extra for, if I didn't mind the stigma. Even if the agency was high-end."

"Wait. Hospital? You were hurt?"

He made a noise that sounded like a laugh, only darker. "Well, I can't protect anyone if I'm not willing to fight. What kind of bodyguard would I be?" His smile didn't reach his eyes.

Cassie couldn't imagine going up against someone like him, as muscular as he was. "What happened?"

"Shot in the gut. Tore through a kidney and a few muscles."

The tight grip on her hand countered the nonchalance in his voice. Every guy had to sound tough when talking about pain, but bodies always told the truth. Muscles remembered pain and tightened to guard themselves. Much like her heart.

"How long ago?"

"About a year."

"Did the guy get away?"

"No," Renner grunted. "But not before he finished off my client and another guard."

"Jesus," she whispered. "Who would do something like that?"

"You can take a gangster out of the ghetto, but not the ghetto out of the gangster. An old grudge gone bad."

"With the means to hire personal security?"

"Well." His heart rate increased under her fingertips. "That's part of the disclosure agreement. Standard security stuff. Can't tell you who, or what they were like."

"Much like the escort business."

A chuckle rumbled in his chest. "The Knight business...very similar."

She caressed his pectoral in small circles with the tips of her fingers. It took a moment to realize she was subconsciously searching for chest hairs. Renner's was smooth. She forced her fingers to stop and just focused on his heartbeat. Strong and steady beneath his bare skin.

His hand closed over her fingers and brought them to his lips. He kissed each one, slowly. Every touch made her heart skip.

"I know you're curious, Cassie." His voice, low and sensual, made the hairs on her neck stand up.

If they weren't covered in darkness, he'd see her blush—

the heat was in her cheeks. Because she was curious. Extremely. She didn't know if she was brave enough.

Brave enough to feel. To want.

To let go.

"You're in the driver's seat." Renner's words were honey across her cheeks. Warmth drifted across the single foot of space between them. Soothing, musky warmth. "I won't make any moves until you do."

A tremor slid down her spine. She took a shaky breath to settle her nerves. Being in the driver's seat was her life right now. Trying to be strong for her son, be a compass in a world flipped sideways, while reining in the overwhelming desire to crumble into a useless heap in the corner.

A tempting, red-horned devil sat on her shoulder, urging her to let go of her reserves and press her lips to Renner's. The haloed, sensible voice in her mind told her the last thing she needed was an opportunity for guilt in an already emotion-filled heart, over capacity.

Tightening her grip on his hand, she curled it under her chin. "Good night, Renner."

She felt him smile—rather than saw it.

"Sleep well, Cassie."

RENNER

"I don't care what you think, those are my fans out there," Renner's client argued from inside the limo. "I can' help it if they want the flava' KingMe's got. Just more money for me." He flashed a gold tooth from the middle of his crooked smile.

"If you'd told me that you informed more of your friends you'd be here, I would've hired more than just two guards. This is unsafe, and I advise we delay your arrival until this thins, or cancel."

KingMe's expression darkened. "You do what *I* say. I'm payin' you to protect me, so do it. I'm going in."

He fought hard to keep from rolling his eyes. "Stay in the car until I clear the area." Renner stepped out and checked his sidearm.

The crowd outside the back door of the concert was much larger than they'd expected. His client's friends had undoubtedly blasted the rapper's whereabouts on social media. Something he'd specifically told the rapper/gangster *not* to do. He already had a big enough target on his chest from the criminal investigation he was involved in for attempted murder, then to add even more attention to his stardom.

The bystanders all wore baggy clothes and heavy coats, making it too easy to conceal a weapon. His private security team didn't have the right to search them either.

The hairs on Renner's arms and neck screamed warnings; this was not a protectable situation. Not to mention the video camera on the corner of the building was dangling from a shredded wire, and half the streetlights were busted. Most of the light was from the dozens of camera phones waiting to capture KingMe's entrance.

He shook his head, and spoke into the microphone in his sleeve. "We need to find an alternate entrance. This one isn't secure."

"The principal insists on going in here, right now," Glicker, the other guard he hired to protect Wilson Rhames, aka KingMe, replied.

The newest cookie-cutter rapper to come out of the shady streets of Chicago, and land a recording deal out of a New York studio. Now here he was in San Antonio, Texas, playing one of the seediest clubs in the state.

Renner bit the inside of his cheek. Professionalism in front of a hundred of his client's fans was required.

Before he had a chance to reply, the limo door opened again, and their over-zealous client stepped out. KingMe flashed his gangster scowl and nodded towards his fans.

They all surged forward to get a closer snap of him.

Glicker raced from around the other side of the vehicle, and he and Renner did the best they could to keep the mob off their principal.

The chaos was insurmountable between keeping the mob off the celebrity and surveying everyone's hands for anything suspicious.

"Move back," Renner barked, not caring if he lost his cool

with an un-protectable situation. *Just get him in the building.*

The door was only fifteen feet away, but KingMe kept pausing to take pictures and flash gang signs.

One sultry female pushed herself in front of him, and lifted her sequined shirt. Revealing her C-cups to KingMe and the rest of the world.

Glicker grabbed the woman's arm to pull her away, but their combative client grabbed her ass and yanked her forward. Their tongues locked, in a loud and slippery French kiss that would've made porn stars gag.

An usher from the concert yanked the doors and held them open.

Ten feet, dammit. Renner leaned over to KingMe. "Bring her in with you, but we have to get off this street. Now."

Without breaking their lips, KingMe flashed him the middle finger, and ground his dick against the girl's crotch.

"Back up!" Glicker shouted at another group of fans.

The woman pulled away from KingMe with a satisfied smile. "Good night, Wilson."

As KingMe blinked and stared at her, Renner dropped his gaze to her hands. Something black and shiny glittered off a camera flash.

His heart stopped, and the world silenced.

He yanked on her arm. A loud bang echoed off the buildings, and Glicker threw himself on their client. Screams followed the echo.

Renner reached for his weapon, and another shot went

off.

More screams filled the air.

Years of training blocked out the image of a female or crazed fan in front of him, and all he saw was the black and white range target. He emptied his mag into the center circle.

She dropped, and her pistol skidded out from under her crumpling body.

The mob dispersed faster than cockroaches in daylight, including trampling over Glicker, who still covered their client on the concrete. Blood spots marred the ground.

Whose blood?

"Get the fuck off me!" KingMe barked.

Glicker didn't move.

Shit. "Glick?"

KingMe shoved the bodyguard off. A small hole dripped blood out of his chest.

His dead eyes glazed up into the sky, and the rapper scurried away on his hands and knees.

"Shit! Is that fucker dead?"

More fans raced away, except for one man who still faced the gruesome scene. With too calm an expression.

"Wilson, run inside!" Renner ordered. "Now!"

"Holy shit!" The rapper continued to stare at Glicker's dead face.

The man reached behind his back.

Renner bent down to pull another pistol from his ankle holster. "Drop it!"

He moved between his client and the suspect, just as the man fired. The bang clashed against the concrete building. Renner fired, hitting the man in the groin.

The man started to drop, but he also managed to fire again.

Renner jerked awake, grabbing his stomach. The room was dark, and there was no pain. Not anymore.

A gentle moan from beside him pulled his attention.

Cassie. Asleep beside him.

A sigh trickled down his body, and he scraped a hand down his face.

The clock glowed *7:30 a.m.* At least he'd had a good night's sleep before the nightmare. His heart was still racing, too fast to hope to go back to sleep. He leaned over and laid a gentle kiss on Cassie's forehead, careful not to wake her.

When his feet hit the wooden floor, the cold seeped into his skin.

Shower. Definitely time for a shower. Wash away those memories.

Chapter
SEVEN

CASSIE

The soft whoosh of the shower woke her from another full night of deep sleep. She stretched under the covers, and glanced at the clock. *7:40 a.m.*

She smiled. Two nights in a row. Almost as good as hot coffee. *Almost.*

Until she crawled out of bed and into the bathroom to see the shower stall's fogged glass. With Renner's toned, muscular everything on full display. Dripping wet.

Yep, I'm awake.

His tanned skin looked darker against the white tiles, except for several scars on his abdomen. Small puncture marks the size of quarters spread out into spider-like webs. Joined by a long, thin white scar. Probably from surgery.

She stood frozen in place, staring. It hadn't occurred to her that he'd take a shower here, even though she remembered offering the first night. When she'd woken, the shower sound must've subconsciously registered as her husband.

Seeing Renner this exposed—it was hard to think.

"Sleep well?"

Her gaze shot to his face, his half-smirk devilishly lopsided. Extremely appealing. He didn't bother covering himself, and her cheeks burned.

Just as her tongue decided to swell, and lose all motor control.

"As I said before," Renner began with that silky voice, "God help any man who sees you at your best. 'Cause that well-rested, cozy morning look on you is heart stopping."

Cassie opened her mouth to speak, but nothing came out.

His eyes lowered for a moment, and his gaze darkened. "If you're cold, I guarantee it's warmer in here."

She looked down and gasped. Her nipples strained against her cotton shirt, traitorous mountains peaked in arousal.

When she looked back at him, so was he.

Fully aroused.

Renner glanced down at himself and rubbed his neck. "He, uh...has a mind of his own. Can you blame him?" A tinge of red graced his cheeks.

She followed her feet out of the bathroom. More like stumbled. Stopping at her door to the hallway, Cassie forced herself to blink. Covering her face was the only way to cool the rising warmth on her skin. Other than dipping her head in a bucket of ice.

Okay, so that part of me is still alive. Good to know.

The image of Renner's hot-as-hell naked body—*wet* body—would be impossible to forget. Forever branded to her memory whenever she thought of the need to pleasure herself. Because after the life with her husband—however short it was—and then that profound display of male masculinity, how could she possibly expect a romantic relationship with anyone else?

Right?

She grabbed a sweater from her dresser and yanked it over her head. Her nipples still screamed their ardent approval of the man-siren in her shower. At least now they wouldn't be as visible. Despite her already overheated body temperature.

He just ruined me. One sultry smile and thirty seconds of in flagrante, and I'm ruined.

An agonizing ten minutes later—and still far too soon— they sat at the breakfast table over steaming coffee. She hardly needed caffeine at this point. Cassie couldn't look at his face. Too embarrassed to see judgment. Or the questions. Or the urge to follow through with her body's retaliation for being dormant so long.

Not ready to let go of...everything.

"I think you've just invented a new shade of red."

She risked a glance into his eyes. As much as she'd

dreaded facing it, his tawny irises only conveyed the same ease and innocence as last night. "What?"

"Too-Hot-For-Coffee."

Cassie circled her hands around her mug, failing to hide a smile. "I think that would better describe you."

Renner laughed. The light-hearted sound lit up the room, then found its way inside her. Even the walls seemed shinier. It'd been a long time since she'd heard that jovial resonance in this house. Full of colors, indeed.

"I didn't mean to make you that uncomfortable," he continued. "When you walked in, there was nowhere to hide. I figured you'd already seen a naked man before, so why bother hiding?"

"There's quite a bit of difference between any naked man and...you." Her cheeks seared again, which she tried to hide behind a sip of coffee.

His smile was so genuine, it hurt. "Thank you."

Her husband had been fit, lean and tone. She'd been attracted to him from the very first day she'd met him their sophomore year of college. But Renner's body—*damn*. The girth had surprised her the most. And smooth skin, well trimmed and...

She bit her lip. "Does it take a lot of effort to keep up that physique?"

He shrugged with one shoulder. "An hour at the gym every day and a good run. An easy regimen to maintain from my military days. Also helps if I limit the fast food trips."

"What was that life like? I'm guessing you're a Marine." A nice segue from the other topic. Something to keep her from this continuous blush and vivid memory.

The smile he gave this time was different. Almost a grimace. "I loved it." Renner's voice dropped. Deeper.

She waited for him to continue, but it took longer than she'd hoped.

"Made some great friends, ones I'll keep my whole life." He paused again. "Lost a few, too." The grip on his mug tightened.

Conversations of lost soldiers, how they died, were very touchy. Most combat men didn't like to talk about it after they came home. Cassie knew that much. She didn't want him to feel that way. Not in her home. These walls had seen enough of that recently.

"I definitely don't miss walking through those sand-covered villages looking for Al Qaeda or ISIS. Those monsters are pure evil. But the Marines taught me how to protect myself. How to protect others. Gave me confidence."

"And purpose."

Renner looked into her eyes, instead of the distant gaze over her shoulders. The grimace faded. "And purpose."

"But you think you've lost that."

He didn't answer. Just sipped coffee.

Then his phone buzzed. He glanced at the screen and the ease on his face switched off. He morphed into business mode. Knight mode. "I need to head out. Have to talk to my boss."

She swallowed the lump in her throat. "Another job?"

The look he gave her was hard to decipher. Discretion, discomfort, insecurity... Cassie blinked and remembered the article she'd read online.

As Renner grabbed the bag of goodies he'd brought, she stood and reached for her purse on the counter. "I forgot to tip you. Here's some cash for—"

"No charge," he interrupted.

She stared.

"You're not a client anymore."

A cold fist gripped her gut, and her lips parted. *He's rejecting me? He doesn't want to see me anymore?* Why did that hurt so much? "Why?"

His deep gaze went straight to her heart. "Because you're something more."

She blinked. Tears that'd formed in her eyes dried instantly. She opened her mouth to reply, but once again nothing came out. *I'm something more. He wants more.* How much more exactly?

The tight squeeze on her stomach released, and her heart felt less heavy.

Cassie followed him to the front door, more on autopilot, because it was still hard to process his statement.

Renner turned at the door. "I'll be here again tonight, if you want me."

She frowned. "Won't I be taking away from your

business?"

"Yes," he replied simply. "See you at seven?"

Cassie nodded, and then realized what he'd said. That she'd said *yes*.

He grabbed his keys from the table and opened the front door.

"Renner?"

He turned. The morning sun caught his eyes in a light that made them almost green. The glow dazzled her. Nearly taking the breath from her lungs. Heat flooded her face.

Just say it. "You are incredibly attractive. Almost too much." *Almost.*

"Thank you." Renner didn't smile this time.

It nearly dissolved her bravery.

But he kept staring. Down into her self-conscious self.

"So are you," Renner breathed. He raised his hand and caressed a strand of her hair. His fingers grazed her cheek. Then cupped her face, his warm calloused hand more comforting than she expected.

Cassie leaned into it, closing her eyes to the soapy scent, fresh and clean. And masculine. The gentle touch of a man, thawing her insides that had been frozen for so long.

His soft lips touched hers, and her heart gasped.

Tender, assertive, but not demanding. Hopeful.

The taste of him was better than she'd imagined. He pulled back too soon, and this time, his face was blushed all the way to his ears.

"See you at seven, Cassie."

Chapter
EIGHT

RENNER

"You're crazy," Renner's boss sighed through the phone, the slight British accent more pronounced when he was angry.

I've said the same thing to myself a thousand times today. "Got a personal thing to handle. Just clear my schedule for the rest of the week, or pass them off to someone else."

"Please, don't tell me this is about that overnight client."

He clamped his teeth together. *Is it that obvious?*

"What did I say when we first met?" Duane's voice turned sharp, and cold. "You don't get involved with clients. The second they get attached, you drop them."

"That's not it, Duane."

Kinda the other way around.

"Then what? You feeling dodgy or something?"

Renner rolled his eyes. Repeating himself was getting on his nerves. "Something in my private life I have to handle."

"Knights don't have a private life, Shaw. The *job* is your

life."

He took a deep breath to calm his rising blood pressure. He remembered their first conversations about becoming a Knight. The time commitment, the physical maintenance and appearance standards, and most importantly the strict protocol of no personal romances interfering with work. All of it seemed like a breeze to his already bachelor lifestyle, the bodyguard experience, and lack of relationships since his return home from overseas.

They'd both made it sound so easy for a Marine like Renner. How so many women had specifically requested the soldier look. His scars were sure to be a huge turn on, they'd said. They'd promised his calendar would be as full as he wanted. He'd never go hungry.

The money aspect depicted was right. There was plenty of dough in this business. It wasn't the cash he was after.

Cassie had pulled the sole motivation out from his soul with the smallest effort.

He wanted a purpose.

Renner wasn't quite sure if she was that purpose, but he knew it was in her direction. He had to devote more time to find out.

"Look, I get it." Duane's voice simmered. "You haven't really had a break since you started. Why don't you take a vacation? I know a guy in Vegas. He'll set you up in a suite. Dorian can go with you. Great place to let off some steam, go out on the lash, and who knows...you might love it there.

Maybe expand the business into new territory. There's huge money in—"

"Duane."

This guy really doesn't listen.

"Huh?"

"I'll call you in a few days." Renner ended the call and shoved the phone in his pocket. After climbing into his truck, he glanced at the takeout bags in the passenger seat. The scent of Teriyaki filled the cabin, and he couldn't wait to dig into the honey chicken. Chinese food. He'd noticed a magnet on Cassie's fridge with the number to a local delivery place. He prayed she'd like this.

Would like him. Out of the Knight role.

His heart hammered against his ribs. He scrutinized his reflection in the rearview mirror. A sheen formed at his hairline just as his belly filled with a swirling sandstorm.

What are you doing? She's a client. You've known her for two days. Don't lose your shit, Renner.

He rested his head on the steering wheel, calming his heart. He'd faced hordes of terrorists with hand grenades and rocket launchers, survived months at a time in scorching deserts with just his field gear and a rifle.

Watched a Humvee full of his friends explode to shreds. Braved countless thugs and would-be murderers as a bodyguard—including the one who'd gotten the drop on him—but at this moment he'd almost prefer staring down that gun barrel again, than face Cassie with his heart in his hands.

She was so much more terrifying.

Is she worth this? He closed his eyes. Her face filled his memory, her smile, her laugh. That incredible tank top and morning-after look that made him hotter than a flash bomb. The way her incredible sea-green gaze looked straight through his analytical façade, and opened him up.

More than anything, her heartache had struck him. Her need to connect to someone, and to feel safe with someone. Even though she fought his attempts so hard.

I can be that someone, if she'll let me.

"Is she worth it?" he said out loud. Renner looked in the mirror. "No guts, no glory."

The clock glowed a bright blue *6:15 p.m.* He was early.

Maybe too early, but it was now or never.

Chapter NINE

RENNER

Renner rang the doorbell at 6:32 p.m., bags in hand. His heartrate jacked, he'd applied an extra layer of antiperspirant and cologne. *Shit, I'm like a frat pledge here.*

The doorknob turned, and he forced a deep breath with his charming smile.

The door swung open, and a pair of brilliant blue eyes blinked up at him. Only four-feet tall, with wavy blond hair and adorably large front teeth.

Renner blinked. Words evaporated, but he couldn't help smiling at the kid. The same soft, oval face and sweet smile as Cassie.

"Who are you?" Such an innocent question out of the small voice, but he didn't know how to answer.

"I'm Renner."

"I'm Landon." The boy looked at the takeout food, and his eyes lit up. "Mommy, the chicken guy is here!" He ran back into the house, his feet clomping on the wood floors.

Renner chuckled. *The chicken guy?*

Cassie came out of the kitchen, phone in hand. Her jaw dropped. "Hi. I...I was literally about to call you."

Her teal shirt hugged her torso in all the perfect places, with only a sliver of cleavage showing. Leaving him with plenty of imagination to remember the plump softness underneath.

Her simple dark jeans were loose around her thighs, but still somehow cradled her waist and butt. And her adorable bare feet begged to be kissed. But with two bags of food and an oblivious five-year-old between them...

Maybe this night is over before it starts.

The boy started jumping up and down, with a huge lopsided grin. "Chicken and rice! Chicken and rice! I'm so hungry! Thank you, Mommy." Landon ran to the kitchen, leaving Cassie with a dumfounded expression.

"I'm sorry," she murmured. "Their camping trip got rained out, and they showed up an hour ago. This is the first chance I've had to call."

"Are your parents here, too?"

"They just left. Come in."

Renner stepped inside, and despite the Chinese food, caught her perfume. Sweet, a touch of floral, and delectably feminine. Her hair was down, loosely curled, and a light layer of eye shadow graced her soft face. Perfectly accentuating the aqua tinge in her green irises.

"Is the chicken guy staying for dinner?" The little boy stood in the hallway, holding a fork and spoon in each hand.

She closed the door behind him and approached her son.

Renner kept his mouth shut, and followed her lead. They'd inadvertently jumped twelve steps forward in the relationship, if that's what they could call it.

"Landon, this is my friend, Renner. He's brought dinner for us. What do you say?"

"Thank you, Renner."

"You like chicken and rice, kid?"

His eyes lit up again. "Yes! It's my favorite!"

Renner followed the boy into the kitchen, tossing Cassie a wink as he passed. The wrinkles on her forehead revealed her unease at the situation.

Time to roll with it.

"Your mom said you went camping."

"Uh huh!" Landon climbed onto one of the stools. "Granddad took me fishing. I caught *four* fish. He showed me how to skin 'em and cook 'em. They tasted awful!"

"Where did you go?"

"Clipper Campgrounds, about an hour away." Cassie filled her plate with teriyaki chicken and brown rice.

"I know that place." He grinned. "Used to go there in Boy Scouts."

"You were in Boy Scouts?" Landon asked, dropping more rice from his spoon than getting in his mouth.

"Long time ago. What did you do up there?"

The kid barely took a breath between sentences as he described his camping trip at warp speed.

Renner was fascinated. As an adolescent, he'd loved camping and learning survival skills in the wild outdoors.

Landon's words brought him right back to his tent-throwing days, building campfires, tracking raccoons, and navigating by the stars.

More importantly, throughout the conversation, Cassie's shoulders had slowly dropped and her smile widened. Finally, her eyes started to glow with a brilliant jade.

It took all his resolve not to grab her hand and kiss her knuckles. Probably not ready for that show of affection in front of her son.

"Granddad said he'd take me again next year. I might be big enough to do the rafting part, too."

"We'll see," Cassie replied.

The sky darkened fast, and rain slowly patted against the windows. A few moments later, it grew to a deluge with a few lightning flashes and rumbling thunder.

"Stupid storm," Landon muttered and lowered a frown to his plate.

"Storms are good, pal." Renner wiped his mouth with a napkin. "Lowers the temperature on hot days, brings new life to the forest, and there's really cool stuff to find in the creek beds."

The little boy looked at him with big round eyes, but didn't say anything.

"Cheer up. You'll get a chance to go back soon." He tossed him a wink, and the boy's frown disappeared. "I can't believe that place is still around. They had awesome wilderness obstacle courses. Zip lines, rope ladders, even a paintball course."

Cassie pointed at Landon, who now wore an envious smile. "Which you're not old enough for. Yet."

He took the last bite of chicken off his plate, and wiped his mouth with his sleeve. "Do you like blueberry muffins?" he asked, still chewing.

Cassie stopped drinking her water mid-sip, and stared at her son.

"Sure do," Renner replied.

"Will you make some with me?" The boy's pleading eyes were wide and bright.

Cassie appeared to be holding her breath.

"Uh...that's up to your mom."

"Can I?" he begged.

"We just finished dinner, sweetie," she said, her obvious concern expanding. The sky outside was now completely dark.

"Please!" Landon whined. "Renner said he likes them. I want to show him how good I am at cooking."

"I don't mind," he whispered to Cassie. "If it's okay with you."

The hesitation she gave him perked up the hairs on his arms.

She bit her lip and sighed. Then finally nodded.

Her son jumped down from the stool, and ran to the cupboard.

"Put your plate in the sink, sweetheart," she called.

As the boy complied, Renner peered into the pantry and stopped. The entire top shelf was full of blueberry muffin mix. Stacked two boxes high. He glanced at Cassie, who seemed to have adopted a permanent expression of self-consciousness.

Roll with it. He grabbed a box.

Landon reached into one of the lower cabinets and pulled out a ceramic mixing bowl along with a few muffin tins.

"You've done this before, huh?"

"Yep. Lots and lots." After they put the ingredients together, Renner grabbed the whisk, but Landon stopped him. "That's my job."

He raised an eyebrow, and handed the boy the whisk. "Have at it."

The kid stirred with a frenzy, dropping powder mix all over the counter. The tongue sticking out of his mouth as he worked was worthy of a Hallmark card.

Renner helped him scoop the batter into the muffin tins, and switched on the oven.

When Landon watched the trays slide in, he grinned. "The next best thing to heaven."

He gave him a smile. The smell was delicious, he'd give that to the little chef. When he turned to Cassie, her eyes had filled with tears, and she kept herself out of Landon's view.

"All right, kid," he announced. "Go wash up. I'll start

cleaning the mess."

"Don't start without me!" Landon ran upstairs, and Cassie beat Renner to his curiosity.

"Thank you for playing along. But you don't have to stay." She wiped her eyes with her sleeve. "I'll clean this. I'm sure you have appointments to make."

"Cassie, look at me."

"Dinner was a huge win," she continued, her voice a little higher. "He loved it. Thank you." She moved back and forth, carrying plates and bowls to the sink and wiping the counter, until Renner grabbed her elbow and gently pulled her to him.

"Relax, just for a minute."

Her pulse raced under his fingers, and her breathing quickened. Not to mention, she kept looking everywhere else but at him.

"He's awesome." Renner smoothed down the goosebumps that had popped up on her arms. "Full of energy."

That dragged a smile from her, however small. But it faded quickly. "He's had a really hard time with everything. I'm glad he's in a good mood."

"Look at me."

With a deep sigh, she finally did. A glisten formed in her eyes again. "You don't have to stay. I understand if this is too much reality for you."

"Cassie, I *want* to be here."

She pressed her lips together. "It's okay, really."

"And miss out on the kick-ass blueberry muffins? No way."

Cassie arched a delicate eyebrow. "Language."

He grimaced. "Sorry. Easy fix."

Landon ran down the stairs in mismatched pajamas with muffin mix still on his face and hands. He carried a picture frame.

"Whatcha got there, bud—" she asked. Her face dropped instantly.

"This is my daddy," the kid announced proudly, and shoved the photo in Renner's face, holding it up on his tiptoes.

His jaw went slack, staring at his blurry reflection in the glass that contained the man's photo. Dark blue eyes, wavy blond hair and easy smile. He swallowed.

Cassie's face had turned white.

Play it cool. Keep it easy. "That's one good lookin' guy." He ruffled the kid's hair. "Just like you."

"His name is Kyle. Did you know my daddy?"

Renner shook his head. "Nope. Did he like blueberry muffins, too?"

The kid grinned into the frame. "Next best thing to heaven."

Then it hit him.

Renner swallowed a gasp and looked at Cassie, who held her arms to keep from shaking. It wasn't working.

The next best thing to heaven.

Landon set the frame on the coffee table and curled up

on the couch.

Renner's heart cracked.

The kid baked blueberry muffins to try and get closer to his dead father. To get closer to heaven. Landon   had to settle for the next best thing.

"He makes those every day, doesn't he?" he asked.

Cassie nodded and turned toward the kitchen. To grab a tissue.

Which explained why the cabinet was full of blueberry muffin mix, top to bottom.

"Renner, will you play a video game with me?" The kid held two remote controls on the couch, propping one out to him.

The innocence of the request, and the cute pleading voice added an extra rip in Renner's heart. "Sure, kid." He sat on the couch beside him, and took the remote. "What do you want to play?"

"Super Mario Brothers. I want to be Luigi. You can be Yoshi."

For the next hour, Landon routinely beat him, one level after another. The boy jumped off the couch in sync with his character, only to plop down on the cushion and tell Renner where to grab the next gold coin, or find a secret tube. With each level, the kid had moved closer and closer to his side.

Only a few times when the mustached character had fallen into a pool of lava, Landon threw a small tantrum. They were over as quickly as they'd started. Every now and then, they'd scarf down a blueberry muffin, tart and scrumptious.

Renner had cast glances at Cassie throughout the game. Permanent creases dug into her forehead. He wanted to swipe them away with his thumb. Or his lips. She'd sat in the side armchair, watching them, instead of the television. A mother's worry never ceased.

Eventually, the video game turned to an animated movie, and shortly thereafter Landon's quiet snore rumbled against Renner's shoulder.

Cassie set her tea mug on the table, and walked over to brush the hair out of her son's face. "He's so tired. I should take him upstairs."

"I can do it." He gave her a smile, hoping she'd relax.

It only made the corners of her mouth turn down. "No, I should."

"It's okay, Cassie," Renner whispered. "He's lighter than flypaper. Sit and enjoy your tea."

She stepped back, reluctance dominating her expression.

He shifted Landon's limp body into his arms, and stood with the boy's head on his shoulder. Still snoring. He carried the matchstick upstairs, remembering his room was the first one on the left. The only sound was the rain pattering against the roofline, soft and soothing.

Gently pushing the stuffed animals and frames to the side of the mattress, he pulled down the covers and laid Landon down. The kid never woke.

Cassie's deceased husband, Kyle, stared at him through a dozen picture frames throughout the boy's room. Memories of a deeply loved man swirled between all these toys, promises from a father to a son dashed, and the idealistic childhood taken away.

"I'm so sorry, kid," he whispered.

With quiet steps, Renner descended the stairs to see Cassie hugging herself and staring out the window. Her shoulders had scrunched up to her mid-neck again. Tense and pale.

He had no idea what to say. There were no words for some things. His first instinct was to wrap his arms around her, make her relax and feel comforted. Everything about her posture said *don't touch me.*

Renner sighed, and shoved his hands in his pockets. And waited. Her eyes caught his gaze in the reflection from the window.

"Thank you," she finally said with a shaky breath. "Those emotional outbursts of his have been happening more often, ever since..."

"Completely expected," he answered for her. "You're doing great."

Cassie blinked several times, and pursed her lips. Probably swallowing her emotions as hard as she could manage. "I don't have the heart to tell him that Clipper Campgrounds will probably close before next spring. This was his last camping trip out there."

Renner shrugged. "There are other camping places around here."

"This was supposed to help him get away from everything. Do something fun."

"It won't be the last time he has fun. Kids are more resilient than you think."

She bit her lip and watched the rain slow to a drizzle. She was only an arm's length away, but the space between them felt as wide as an ocean.

As he watched the storm of emotions fill her body, he desperately wanted to find a way to cross that ocean, pull her out of it.

To be happy.

"Do you want me to stay, Cassie?"

Her pause clawed at his heart. What hurt worse was that she didn't even look at him. The word *no* was only a heartbeat away.

Whenever she said it, Renner's stomach would swallow him whole.

"Yes. Until I fall asleep," she finally replied, her eyes full of hope.

Chapter TEN

CASSIE

Sleeping in Renner's arms on the couch confirmed the feelings she'd been swallowing. He had a magical way of settling her. Pulling together her frazzled nerves, and waking her up from her depressive spiral. He forced her to see the colors in life.

There was no denying it.

Breathing him in throughout the night was like an opiate. More than just taking the edge off—he chased the storms away.

Two things bothered her.

First, was it *Renner* who made her feel like this, or just someone filling a space? A need. A body to cushion herself against, to take the place of Kyle, even only temporarily. If that were even possible.

Second, any kind of relationship was too soon. Deep in the back of her mind, a nagging voice wouldn't shut up.

Too soon.

Give yourself time to grieve.

Yet the human spirit could only take so much darkness before the internal lantern would snuff out. Every now and then, the light had to be refueled. Cassie had been crawling through a black tunnel the last six months, running on residual light gained from energy drinks and late night memories.

At some point, the rain had started again and pelted the roof and windows. She cuddled deeper into his arms, his body warm and strong against hers. The rain lulled her to a drowsy doze. Until Renner's hard-on pushed against her bottom. She shifted, but it only lengthened and grew harder. And warmer.

He inhaled, slow and deep, and pressed into her.

Is he still asleep?

Then his arms wrapped around her, hugging her, with one large palm covering her breast. Even through her clothes, her skin flamed.

A hot swirl pooled low in her gut, then moved to between her thighs.

Even in his sleep, he knows how to arouse a woman.

"Renner?" she whispered.

He didn't answer.

Cassie pressed her lips together, and tried to turn in his arms, to shimmy out from underneath him. When she made it to her back, his grip tightened and he groaned, low and sultry in her ear. The sound caressed her skin.

Renner burrowed his lips against her temple, laying soft, sleepy kisses on her skin. Her heart fluttered.

She turned her head to say something, to wake him. His mouth instantly covered hers. His tongue grazed along her upper lip, then suckled it between his teeth. Along with sucking the gasp from her lungs.

Oh God, the taste of him. Sweet, spicy, and ridiculously hot. Her mouth involuntarily opened for him. Before she knew it, she was kissing him back with everything she had. Her leg wrapped around his knee, and her hand caressed up his neck. His short hair felt like feathers under her fingertips.

She had no idea she'd wanted him this bad.

From her racing heartbeat, fiery cheeks, and throbbing center, clearly her body screamed for it. At this point, her subconscious didn't care if he was still asleep, and acting out a dream.

She certainly was.

His weight shifted over her, his body like a heavy, comforting blanket. The rigid length between his legs pressed against the junction of her thighs.

Everything pulsed. Her head, her heart, and especially her sex. His hand slipped under buttocks, and he squeezed, pulling her harder into his frame.

Simultaneously, his tongue dived deeper into her mouth, licking every crevice. Cassie moaned against him, and dragged her fingernails down his scalp.

Renner growled, the vibrations echoing down her throat.

They resonated through her chest.

Lightning flashed, but thunder didn't register in her mind. All she could hear was his moan and the adrenaline rushing her ears. Her body sparked, as if it could feel color. The hot reds, intense pinks, and the delicious hazel of his eyes.

His eyes. They were open now. Staring down into her, watching her body react. Writhing and squirming, begging for more.

She reached down and grabbed a handful of his ass, grinding his pelvis into hers.

His tongue grazed along her cheek to her ear, and devoted his expert attention to her lobe. Renner's hot breath on her neck swirled the insane colors over her head in tandem with more lightning, dancing across the ceiling.

Her head fell to the side, and she bit her lip.

His hand moved up, underneath her shirt and settled over her breast. His palm massaged the straining peaks against her bra.

Everything was so intense, so dizzying, she nearly burst right then.

Another streak of lightning illuminated the room.

Looking back at her from the picture frame on the coffee table was Kyle's face. Where her son had left it, next to the plate of blueberry muffin crumbs.

Cassie gasped. She nearly choked on a half-scream.

Renner's head shot up, and he lifted his weight from her body. "Did I hurt you?"

Shame stole the power from her voice, so she shook her head. The image of her dead husband's face staring at her while she nearly lost control with another man might as well have been a truck load of ice burying her alive.

Mortified didn't even begin to cover it.

Cassie shoved herself up from the couch, pushing Renner off and onto the cushions. Anything to get out from underneath him. Away from the incriminating scene. She covered her face as she escaped to the corner of the room.

"What's wrong?" His cheeks flushed with arousal. He stood from the couch, sporting a thick erection pushing against his jeans.

One she'd encouraged. One she'd nearly given in to.

Humiliation clawed at her throat, swallowing her words. Until she didn't have to say anything, because he looked down at the photo on the table.

"Oh shit," Renner whispered.

The ultimate 'oh shit.' Cassie hugged herself, her skin now covered in goosebumps, and her body shaking.

"It's okay, Cassie," he cooed. He grabbed the frame and moved it to the kitchen, setting it face down on the counter. Then he switched on the overhead lights.

"Turn them off," she squeaked. "Turn off the lights!" She couldn't bear to see his face. To be seen like this, on the wake of a disrespectful act.

"It's just a picture." His voice was soft, an attempt at soothing, but it was the last thing she felt. "He's not here."

"Yes, he is," she croaked. "He was just here. I swear I felt him."

The grimace that flashed on Renner's face was a mixture of disgust and agony. "That was me. You felt me."

"You need to go." Cassie croaked, and her throat closed in on itself.

He shook his head. "Don't do this. Don't shut me out."

"Go!" she breathed. More like wheezed. Then, it was hard to inhale, and her chest caved in on itself. Her fists clenched, and her vision narrowed to a dark tunnel.

She pushed her back against the wall, to brace herself.

Slowly, Renner's image slid, and she looked up at him from the floor.

His lips moved, but she couldn't hear a thing.

Chapter
ELEVEN

RENNER

Another anxiety attack. This time it was one hundred percent his fault. His twisted stomach wouldn't let him forget it.

Cassie had slid down the wall, her body completely closed off. Her eyes glazed over, and everything about her turned rigid.

He called her name, lifted her stiff form to the couch and began the routine of opening her up. Her hands, her arms, her jaw. All the while, swallowing the debilitating embarrassment of getting caught by her former husband's picture.

Renner had never done that—felt up a woman in his sleep. Started something his body desperately wanted to finish, without his mind knowing. He hadn't even been fully awake and aware of what was happening, until Cassie had scraped her fingers down his scalp. That woke up him, and sent his dick into overdrive. It'd been impossible to take his eyes off her.

She was so alive. So passionate. So heartbreakingly beautiful.

So much better than the other dreams—nightmares— that had plagued him for months.

Dammit, he'd never wanted a woman more.

Then it hit him. Was she even awake? Was she dreaming? Imagining her husband, only to realize *he* wasn't Kyle?

He shook his head. Her eyes had been open at that point, in the middle of their almost-consummation, staring back at him. She had to have known.

This was about the picture frame.

Slowly, Cassie's body relaxed, and her eyes registered him sitting next to her.

"Hey there." It was the only thing he could think of to say.

So stupid.

"Where's Landon?" Her voice was airy, and exhausted.

"Still sleeping."

Cassie sat up and flexed her fingers. Then she dragged her hair away from her face. Her gaze landed on everything in the room, except Renner.

He swallowed down the disappointment, more painful than he'd expected.

"What time is it?" she asked.

"Almost four a.m."

"How long...this time?" She still refused to look at him, now hugging herself and staring at the carpet.

"Just a minute." His erection still raged, in full retaliation against his mind. "Have you talked to someone about medication? Anti-anxiety or something? You know, with a professional?"

"You mean, like you?" Her voice cut him hard.

I thought we'd already crumbled those stereotypes.

She winced. "Sorry. I'm not angry at you."

"You're beating yourself up. But you don't have to."

Cassie sighed, and he could feel her pulse accelerate just sitting beside her. The whole room tensed again. She turned her head toward him, but she still didn't look him in the eyes. Her own turned glassy. "You need to go," she whispered.

His heart squeezed in on itself. Renner reached for her hand, the one that'd been gripping her thigh. She pulled away, and his heart shredded. "Are you sure you're not going to have another panic attack?"

"Thank you for everything, Renner. You don't know how much what you've done has meant to me." She stood and went to the hallway. "But this is over."

He tightened his jaw. "You're seriously going to torture yourself over being attracted to another man?"

Cassie didn't respond. She didn't need to. She was locking herself up, and shutting down.

After he'd opened her up to the possibility of something else. Something new.

The connection between them had been unmistakable. At least, in his mind. They'd sparked. To the point where everything had become clear, and the woman standing in front of him, this incredibly strong, resilient, loyal, hot-as-hell woman was the only one Renner could see himself wanting.

"Please, tell me you felt it." His voice was barely more than a murmur. Because any louder, and she might shut down completely. "Tell me that connection was there for you. Because I've never felt that instant click before with anyone."

And you're about to rip it away from me.

She swallowed, and her cheek muscles flexed. Like she was biting back a response, hard.

His shoulders sagged. She wasn't ready. Letting go of her husband's memory wasn't something she could do. He sighed. More as a way to keep from dissolving at her feet.

Renner stood, grabbed his keys from the counter and strode past her to the front door.

Her silence cinched his heart.

He opened the door, but stopped at the darkened, puddled walkway. He closed the door and turned to her.

Her face lifted to his, her eyes glassy.

"I'm just going to say it, because I know I'll never get the chance again. We've only known each other, what, three days? But I've fallen in love with you, Cassie."

Her eyes widened, just as a tear fell to her cheek. She quickly wiped it away, and still didn't respond.

Renner shrugged. There was no other explanation. "I've

never been more sure of my feelings than right now. And it's terrifying. I have no clue if you feel the same way, but none of that matters, does it? Because I met you too late."

Cassie started to tremble.

He desperately wanted to walk over and hold her against him. Breathe in her sweet scent, and show her a life full of color, laughter and love. But he glued his feet to the floor. "In another time, another life, I would've asked you out to dinner. And then more." Her pained smile tore his heart further. Because he meant every word. "I want more with you. Much more. But you can't even admit you want someone else. That it's *okay* to want someone else. Not until you're ready to let him go."

"Renner," she whispered.

He glanced over his shoulder.

Her cheeks were wet, and she took a shaky breath. "You met me too soon."

A lump caught in his throat. "Let me know when you're ready to start that new life. If you want me."

The infernal knocking on the front door to Renner's apartment didn't stop for a full minute. Despite his best attempts to ignore it by covering his head with the pillow.

The raging headache after downing a bottle of Tennessee Red was an ominous sign of the rest of the day.

It wasn't nearly as bad as the pain in his chest.

The kick was that the liquor had failed to chase away the nightmares, too.

"Renner, it's Dorian." His friend's muffled voice made him groan. "Open up."

"Go away," he screamed at the door, and instantly regretted it. The pounding seared through his brain.

"It's five o'clock, man. When did you turn into a vampire?"

"I don't care what time it is."

"Don't make me use the spare key, man. Duane asked me to check on you. Said you were talking squirrelly."

Only a pansy man would use the word *squirrelly*. Renner threw the covers over his head, praying Dorian would leave.

The unmistakable sound of a key turning in his lock made him cuss.

"Shit, man. Did you bring the party back to your place or something? You got a girl in there?"

The only girl I want, won't have anything to do with me.

"Come out here, shithead. I don't want to see your naked ass in that bed."

"Then leave." He forced himself up anyway. Renner threw on a t-shirt and a pair of workout shorts. He scraped his fingers through his hair, willing the pounding to end.

Painkillers. I definitely need painkillers.

He could hear Dorian scrounging around the kitchen for something. By the time he'd left his room and turned the corner, Dorian already had a plastic cup of water on the counter for him, with two pills beside it. The hard-ass stare on his old Marine buddy matched well with his pristine suit and tie. Complete with rough stubble on his face.

Most women swooned over the dark, devilish look, but only made him want to punch the asshole. "What're you doing here?"

Dorian nodded at the empty bottle of whiskey. "Figured you'd need these after you clearly destroyed that precious puppy."

Renner downed them.

"What's her name?" he asked, leaning against the counter with his arms crossed.

He glared. Then got more water.

"You weren't this messed up after your principal got killed. Has to be about a woman."

Renner threw his cup in the sink. "Why the hell would you bring that up?"

"Bury yourself in work. That's the trick."

"Not if former friends keep talking about it."

Dorian threw him a smile, then moved to the living room. "Get dressed, pal. My client's friend needs a date. Totally into jarheads."

Renner pinched the bridge of his nose. "Pass."

His friend put the empty whisky bottle and glass into the sink, and started straightening up the place.

"Stop this shit. You're not my maid."

"No, but we're in a hurry, and I know you. Can't leave your house until everything is in its place."

"I'm *not* going, Dorian."

"They're paying double the rate. Formal event downtown. Pick out a suit, let's go."

"I'm out."

His buddy stopped picking up, and stared. "What? At the dry cleaners or something?"

Renner shook his head. "I'm done. I'm turning in my cufflinks. This job isn't for me."

Dorian's brow furrowed, and he shoved his hands in his pockets. "It's always a woman that does it."

"I appreciate you helping me out after all that mess. But I need to do something else."

The guy's frown gave him a vicious aura, but only because of the stubble and dark suit. His friend didn't have a violent bone in his body, unless he was holding a rifle on tour overseas. "I know this role takes an adjustment. But it's not the traditional escort agency. Being a Knight is more...substantial. Your heart is in the right place, man. It just takes time."

"There's not enough time in the world for me to forget this. Find someone else."

Dorian's frown deepened, but there was a small acquiescence in his stare. "Then at least come as my friend, tonight. I need a wingman."

Renner bit the inside of his cheek. He was on the verge

of shaking his head.

"Murphy," Dorian added.

He sighed. "Of course, you'd use that." Their code word for a personal favor, man to man. Soldier to soldier. After their friend, Murphy, had taken six bullets in the back in Afghanistan while covering their cherry asses during an evac that'd become a slaughterhouse. No one from their unit said it unless they really needed backup. "As a friend. Nothing more."

Twenty minutes and a shower later, Renner reluctantly splashed on aftershave. He hadn't put much effort into his hair this time, and he'd grabbed his least favorite tie. A fitting sentiment for the night.

He grabbed his black stone cufflinks, and scowled as he put them on. Then he slipped on his coat.

Dorian started talking from the living room.

"Are you speaking to yourself out there?" Renner called. "Cause I can't hear a word."

"Renner, you have a guest."

He came out of the bathroom, and turned the corner.

Then froze.

His buddy held open the door, with Cassie in the entryway. Slack jawed.

Chapter TWELVE

CASSIE

Cassie took a deep breath, steeling her resolve.

If you're watching, Kyle, please don't. I can't do this with you in my head.

The door swung open, and a pristine black suit and tie stood in the doorway.

Not Renner.

This man was several inches shorter than Renner, dark brown eyes and six o'clock shadow. Just as ridiculously handsome, in a more rugged way. She glanced at the apartment number again. "Sorry, I must have the wrong address." *Unless he has a roommate.*

"Who ya lookin' for?" Suit-and-Tie gave her a half-smile, his eyes twinkling.

"Renner Shaw."

His smile turned sad. "Well, that explains a lot."

Cassie cocked her head.

He opened the door wider. "You've got the right place. I'm Dorian, friend of Renner's." He put out his hand. When she shook it, he turned her palm downward, and covered her knuckles with his other hand. "Such a shame. We could've had a beautiful relationship." He finished with a dashing smile.

She smirked.

"Are you speaking to yourself out there?" Renner's voice called from somewhere inside. "Cause I can't hear a word."

"Renner, you have a guest." Dorian let her step inside. "Don't break his heart," he muttered.

Her heart rate kicked up a notch, and she pressed her lips together. Break *his* heart?

Renner came around the corner, freshly shaven in a black suit with onyx and silver tie. And dripping with magnetism.

Her jaw dropped. That getup almost guaranteed instant orgasms with just one glance.

"Cassie?" His eyes were wide, hopeful. Tugging at her soul.

Her fingers desperately wanted to caress that smooth face. Run them through his hair, more wild and untamed than she'd seen before. "Well, dammit. This isn't fair."

He's going on another date.

Another client.

She bit her lip, and her chest twisted. Stick to the plan.

"How did you know where I—"

"You left your wallet." Cassie pulled the brown leather

from her purse, willing her hands to stop shaking.

"Oh." Renner's face fell, along with the light in his eyes. He took the wallet. "Thanks."

The pause drifted to an uncomfortable lull. She should turn away, go home. Her feet were fused to the floor.

Renner looked too good to tear her eyes away.

"This is my friend, Dorian." A blush ran up Renner's cheeks. "Come in."

"Actually, I just came to..." *To what? Don't you remember?*

"This looks a lot more intense and...complicated than I want to handle." Dorian broke in. "So, I'll head out. Renner, call me later. Nice meeting you, Cassie." He closed the door behind him, leaving them to stare at each other.

"Where did I leave it?" Renner finally asked, breaking the awkward silence.

"Landon found it between the couch cushions." *Where we groped each other and almost...* Her face heated.

"Where is he?" he asked.

"Landon? A friend's house."

"Can I get you a drink?"

"No, this'll just take a minute." *Do it, Cassie. Say what you came to say, and get the hell out of here.* She took a deep breath. "Can you take off that suit coat? I can't do this when you look like that."

"Like what?"

"Like a walking orgasm."

114

He chuckled. So, he took off the coat and draped it over a chair. "Better?"

The shirt framed his torso too well, and the black and silver tie too elegant a style. Then he stuck his hands in his pockets, accentuating the tightness of his pants around the crotch.

"Nope."

"Well, you couldn't talk to me with my shirt off last time, so this'll have to do." Renner took a step toward her, like a panther.

"You're clearly on your way to a client. I don't want to delay you from your work."

He shook his head. "That's not what—"

"I came to say goodbye." Cassie tightened her grip on her purse.

He stopped, and his shoulders dropped.

The hard part was next.

She was grateful for his silence, but not the oncoming long face. "I couldn't admit this last night. But you're right, there's a connection between us. I felt it. And it terrified me. Because I was scared of what that meant."

Renner's jaw flexed.

Those delectable hazel eyes bored into hers with a heat that she desperately wanted to taste, but she couldn't. Her heart raced, and it was too hard to get a deep breath. "I want you, Renner. God knows how badly I do."

He took another step toward her, but she backed up and

shook her head.

"Stop."

He did.

Thank God.

"It took a lot for me to admit it. Despite all that, I can't do this. My heart is still with him." Her voice broke and she swallowed hard. "I don't know if I'll ever get it back."

His expression turned to pity. Or heartache. It was hard to tell. "You came here to tell me that?"

"You deserved to hear this in person. You needed to know the truth, but I don't want you to wait for me, either. Because I don't know if I'll ever be able to love anyone else again. Not like that. That's not fair to you."

Renner looked away, studying the carpet in the dining room. After a deep sigh and rubbing his chin—that freshly shaven face worth stroking—his gaze met hers. "He's a memory, Cassie. Yes, a great memory, one that's hard to let go of. One you'll always be thankful for. But, he's a *memory*, Cass. I'm standing right in front of you."

Tears pricked her eyes, and she blinked them back. *Then why do I still feel him?* Her heart tightened.

"I know he was a great guy," Renner continued. "I can tell by the way you talk about him. Probably the best you'd ever known. You still want him back. The truth is, I was wrong yesterday. Kyle *is* still here. In Landon."

At the sound of her son's name, the lump crawled into her throat. More tears climbed forward.

"He's the cutest kid I've ever seen." His gaze penetrated the heaviest part of her soul, and she swore she saw a touch of glass in his eyes. "I know it's not the same, but it's the next best thing." His voice scaled higher, the pleading more painful than she anticipated.

Her own stomach was on the verge of collapse.

"You can have the next best thing to him, Cassie," he continued. "You can have blueberry muffins with your son every morning, and me at your side. Do I know for sure it's going to work? No. There are no guarantees in life. Dammit, I want to give it a try. I'll make those blueberry muffins with both of you every day. As long as you love me for *me*, not for the sake of a rebound. Someone you *settled* on."

Everything inside her ached, and Cassie doubted that her lungs could inflate.

How am I still standing?

"I can't bring him back. I can't replace him. No one can. But I can respect him by loving his son. By loving you, with everything I have. I'm envious he met you before I did. But you have to let him go, Cassie. You have to be *willing* to let go. Because I won't live life in a shadow. I can't compete with a ghost."

She bit her tongue to keep from sobbing, but a tear finally fell. Choose between the memory of, and honoring her husband, or the man standing in front of her. So attractive, alive, and full of color. Who gave her the first night of peace in forever.

"You're not ready to do that." Everything in Renner's posture turned to resignation. "Because you're so loyal and loving. And I love you even more for that."

Finally, his charm won the battle over her inhibitions.

Cassie surged forward and placed her tear-covered lips to his. Without any control, her hands stroked his face, the smooth skin stealing more of her breath.

He wrapped his arms around her, his hands sliding up her back in a possessive, intoxicating claim. His tongue glided into her mouth, and she savored him.

Utterly delectable, and completely gut-shattering.

Renner stepped forward, pushing her against the door, and pressed his chest into her breasts. Making it that much harder to breathe.

Oxygen is overrated anyway.

"Don't lock yourself away into that black box," he whispered between ground-shaking kisses. "You deserve that intense kind of love." His hands roamed lower, around her waist, then her hips. "Every minute, of every day. Because you're *more* than worth it."

Her purse fell to the floor, and she gripped his collar. The entire evening flashed in front of Cassie. Devouring each other right here on the floor by the door. Then to the couch. Or the dining room table. Certainly multiple rounds in the bedroom. With his hypnotizing cologne, expert mouth, and damn, those hands—she'd love every second of it. *Of him.*

She tugged him in closer, and the diamond on her finger

dug into her skin. Which instantly cooled the heat in her face. Cassie pulled back, and pressed her hand against his sternum to stop him.

His shaky breath fell against her face, and he covered her hand with his.

"Thank you," she panted. "For loving me. But I'm sorry."

The hazy look in his eyes cracked. Renner's hands dropped.

Tears pricked her eyes again, and she blinked them away.

He'd admitted to falling in love with her, and she was throwing it in his face.

As gently as possible, but it was still a rejection.

Just as painful for her, too. Probably for Kyle, too.

"You'd be living your life always compared to a memory. One I can't let go of yet."

Renner took a shaky breath, and stepped back. The distance between them was only a foot, yet might as well have been a mile. His gaze lowered to the floor. It was a long moment before he looked at her.

Much longer than she wanted.

"One day you will." He shoved his hands in his pockets again, and sighed. "You don't want to hear that right now, but one day. You will love again, deeply. And you should. Because you're incredible." He gritted his teeth and shook his head. "Dammit, I wish like hell it was with me."

Cassie's lungs wouldn't expand to breathe. The words

rested on her lips, *me too.*

She picked up her purse, swallowed her twice-broken heart, and left.

Chapter
THIRTEEN

RENNER

"Are you ready to go?" Dorian crossed his arms, the muscles in his arms bulging forward. He leaned against the black Charger, his pride and joy.

Renner stared down the street, in the direction where Cassie had ridden off. With his heart. He shook his head.

"I assumed with Miss Sainthood leaving, you'd changed your mind."

He shoved his hands in his suit pockets. They felt heavier, and less capable than an hour before. He shook his head again.

"Then what do you want to do?"

Another car drove down the street, a white sedan, that slowed as they continued past him. A window rolled down, and a woman whistled.

Dorian smiled back, but it wasn't his genuine one. Wearing their black suits definitely drew more attention, and

Knights were always on the lookout for new clients.

Not Renner.

He couldn't even lift his gaze enough to look at the catcallers. Let alone react.

"It'll be a fun a party." His buddy crushed a rock under his foot. "Free drinks, and plenty of pretty ladies to take your mind off things. Besides, I need a spotter."

"I said no." The words came out harshly, but he didn't have the capability to be charming right now. "Don't you dare Murphy me on this. Not this one."

Dorian frowned further. "I'm sorry, man. Wrong place, wrong time, huh?"

He nodded absently. "Story of my life."

"No. With your luck? That would be right place, wrong time. Irish, through and through."

"Semantics." Suddenly, the only thing Renner wanted to do was punch something. His fists tightened, so he crossed his arms. To prevent accidentally punching Dorian. Or his car.

His friend slipped on his sunglasses. "Don't make any decisions tonight. Sleep on it. Have a clear head first."

He shook his head. "I've made up my mind. I'm not you, D."

His buddy sighed. "With a woman like that, I get it. I'm not gonna tell you you're making a mistake, like Duane would. No matter what you decide, you owe the man at least a phone call. I'm won't be your messenger boy."

"Fine," Renner growled.

He opened the car door. "Plenty of fish in the sea, but you won't catch any if you just sit around playing with your rod."

Renner glared.

"Loosen up, John Snow. Since when did you become such a boy scout?"

Chapter FOURTEEN

RENNER

Eleven Months Later

A caravan of cars pulled up the long, dirt drive. Renner stood on the main log cabin's front porch, his sunglasses perched on his nose and hands behind his back. The cars stopped, and out climbed his principals.

Very important guests to guard with his life. For the whole weekend.

A dozen grinning kids piled out of minivans and SUV's, each with pristine uniforms and overloaded backpacks.

Not pristine for long.

Several dads and a few moms gathered more gear from the trunks, and corralled behind the boys.

"Welcome, Troop 155!" he called.

They cheered, all lining up at the bottom of the porch steps, with their eager faces looking up at him. This was his favorite age. Six and seven year olds. So open to learning, and loving the silly side of life. Too young to worry about being cool or bugged by peer pressure, but old enough to appreciate the luxury of getting dirty.

"You guys look awesome! Are you ready to earn your survival badges?"

"Yes!" they screamed.

"You better be, or I'll sic the bears on you." A few scared faces blinked at him, while others grinned.

A few parents chuckled.

Renner smiled. "These bears." He turned and motioned to Max, who carried a large basket of teddy bears in Boy Scout uniforms. "These ferocious animals will be waiting for you at the end of the trip, with your badges attached to their sashes."

A few boys clapped, others cheered. From their shuffling feet, he could tell they were anxious to get started. So was he.

"I'm Renner Shaw, and this is Max Fogle. We're your guides for the weekend. By the end of this trip, you will all know how to survive in the wilderness. Survival skills including starting a campfire, pitching a tent, tracking animals, and reading a compass. For extra fun, you'll have the chance to earn a bonus badge for star navigating."

One boy with black hair in front waved his hand. "Will we learn how to shoot?"

"Yes!"

A few parents looked at each other, their smiles instantly vanished.

"With a bow and arrow," Renner amended. "Archery. Another badge opportunity."

"Sweet!" The kid gave his friend a high-five.

"Are you a soldier?" another child asked from the back.

Renner raised an eyebrow. "Why do you ask?"

"Cuz you look like one."

Max chuckled behind him. "What does a soldier look like?"

"Really short hair, big boots, and big arms. Just like yours."

He chuckled. *Who can argue with that logic?* "Yes, Max and I were both Marines. Now, are we ready to get started?"

They cheered again, and everyone followed him over to the lake, where they'd start with putting up their tents and going over the rules.

An hour later, Renner helped a young scout light the kindling for his campfire. When the first embers sparked to life, the smile on the boy's face filled him with internal warmth.

"Renner." Max came over carrying some sticks. "A few stragglers just showed up. Can you check them in?"

"Yeah, I'll take care of it. Sam," he turned to the scout. "Show Max how big this campfire is going to be." He winked.

Cottonwood blossoms on the ground softened his steps, the remnants of a warm spring fading away, and welcoming the summer heat. However, a cool breeze promised at least one more semi-chilly evening. The blooms rose in the air around his head, and he turned the corner at the main cabin.

"Mom, they've already started," a young voice called, one vaguely familiar. A boy ran around the silver SUV. Blond hair and blue eyes, sporting a crisp scout uniform.

"Landon?" he muttered, almost to himself.

The boy stopped, and smiled.

"Landon, honey, wait for me." The SUV door shut, and a woman appeared.

The woman.

Her glorious sunshine hair was held back by dark shades on her head. Shimmering forest-green eyes—like the trees over their heads—stared at him, her mouth agape.

"Cassie." Her name came out like a melody, two syllables he'd barely uttered in eleven months. Too painful to say, but he'd dreamed about her constantly.

"Renner!" Landon ran over to him. The kid was so tall, and he was growing into cheeks. "Are you here for the Cub Scout campout, too? Where've you been?"

He remembers me? "Uh...I've been here. You look awesome, buddy."

The boy beamed and grabbed his sash. "I've got six badges already. Wanna see?"

Renner couldn't take his gaze away from Cassie. The light in her eyes accentuated the astonishment on her face.

"What are you doing here?" Her arms were full of gear, pulling her light blue, buttoned shirt tighter at her breasts. The pink tinge to her cheeks gave off an angelic aura.

"This is my place."

Cassie glanced at the log cabin. "Clipper Campgrounds?"

"I bought the property last year."

Her eyes widened, and those luscious pink lips of hers looked as if they tried to form words, but nothing came out.

"Here, let me help you with that stuff." Renner surged forward and grabbed a few bags off her shoulders, and pulled the cooler behind him.

She absently walked beside him, looking between him and her son running ahead to join his friends. The fresh, plum scent from her hair filled the air.

"Are you still...with the agency?"

"I quit."

Cassie blinked. Then a smile graced her face. Breathtaking.

"What about you?" he asked. "Have you been seeing anyone?"

She paused and inhaled.

"Cassie! So glad you could join us." Their troop leader came around his half-constructed tent. "Where's Clyde?"

"He got stuck at work this weekend. A big case landed on his desk."

"Bummer," the troop leader's dropped tone was genuine. "Come set up over here. Landon's already dropped off his bag."

Renner's stomach crumpled in on itself at the mysterious *Clyde*.

She's dating someone.

He followed Cassie to the other side of the campfire, pretending to be unaffected by the realization that she was not only seeing someone, but said-someone was supposed to be here this weekend.

Perhaps he should be grateful that the guy wouldn't be here. Tormenting his grief.

Renner dropped the bags by Landon's backpack, and forced himself to put on his survival-guide face. *She's a client.* "Go ahead and set up your tent. We'll start the nature hike shortly."

"Thanks." Her eyes pleaded with him to stay. "Where are you—"

"I'll be back in a minute." He had to step away. Staring into those eyes, knowing they looked at someone else with the affection he'd wanted so badly—had dreamed of countless nights—ripped him apart.

After all this time, his feelings hadn't even dulled. Which became perfectly clear to him the second he'd seen her.

He had to regroup. Refocus.

The cottonwood blossoms flattened under his feet as he retreated to the main cabin. The torment was worse because she looked so amazing. Her hair was longer, with new strawberry highlights layered in. Her curves had an additional fullness to them, no longer as thin as a toothpick. Even more attractive than before, if that were possible.

Happiness looked good on her.

So be happy for her.

He'd predicted she'd find someone and love again. Too bad he was right.

Renner went straight to the supply cabinet, and pulled out an extra med kit, a few bottles of insect repellent, and his whistle. Lastly, he grabbed the scavenger hunt lists.

A dozen boys would find bird's nests, deer tracks, acorns, certain flowers and berry bushes, and various other items on a hunt that would take most the afternoon. The hunt finished its trail leading them to a special treasure chest. Full of the materials they'd need to make s'mores this evening, along with a bunch of small toys.

He placed his hands on the counter. Grounding himself to the task was the first step. This new job Renner loved had to be his main priority. He'd been looking forward to this survival group for weeks.

The first major reservation of the season, and he'd gone all out to make it extra special.

So make it special for them. For Landon.

"Do you have any insect repellent?"

He looked up. Cassie stood in the doorway. He hadn't even heard her hiking boots clomp up the steps. The clean and shiny rubber soles had probably never been worn before. Also looking brand new were those jeans. Curvy and form-fitting along every inch of her long legs.

"Landon left his at home," she added with a smile.

Renner swallowed. "Sure." He reached into the supply

cabinet and grabbed an extra bottle for her. "When did Landon join Cub Scouts?"

She stepped forward, her hands behind her waist. "Right after you mentioned *you* were in Boy Scouts."

He stared. "Seriously?"

Cassie nodded, the adorable smile forming a small dimple on her cheek.

"Good for him." He set the bottle on the counter.

She leaned her elbows on the edge, taking and rolling the spray between her fingers.

"You should use some, too. That perfume of yours will attract every mosquito in the park."

Cassie nodded, and then pressed her lips together. "When did you quit the agency?"

He closed the cabinet and locked it. "That night."

Her gaze shot to his face. Her piercing green eyes widened. "You didn't find your purpose there?"

"Actually, I did."

She cocked her head to one side, and her eyebrows furrowed.

Renner smiled. "You reminded me of something I loved once. Something I was good at."

"You seem very good at multiple things." The corner of her mouth lifted.

He chuckled. Her implication wasn't missed. Not that he liked to brag about it, but he liked to think he could please a woman to keep her wanting more. Well, except one. The one that mattered. "When you mentioned Clipper Campgrounds that night, a little light switched on in my mind. A few months later, I dug into my savings, joined in with my buddy, and bought the property."

Her eyes shimmered in the light from the window.

"In a way." He crossed his arms across his chest. "You helped me find my purpose. So, thank you."

Cassie's stare, intent and focused, lasted longer than he expected. "You're welcome."

He forced a sigh. "How's life?"

She paused again. Unsettling, and equally mesmerizing. "Full of color."

The comment should have lifted his spirits, and he almost smiled. But it was hard to hold back the grimace. "With Clyde?"

Her smile flickered. "Clyde?"

"The guy you're seeing. I'm happy for you." If Renner said it enough times to himself over the weekend, he might actually believe it.

Cassie blinked, and then stifled a laugh. "My brother."

He paused. "Oh." He blinked, and inhaled. "I assumed you were—"

"No." She smiled and straightened, still holding the insect repellent. "My brother volunteered to take Landon to den meetings every week. Ever since my son joined Cub Scouts, he's been a happier kid. Helped him through his grief."

"Good." Renner nodded. "He deserves to be happy."

"So, I should thank *you* for that."

He shrugged, more to keep his nerves from unraveling. Being this close to her, and those incredible lips of hers, frayed the rope around his restraint. Her intoxicating scent would drive him mad. Renner tightened his arms, inadvertently flexing his biceps. "You deserve to be happy, too."

She sighed, and the pink in her cheeks reddened. "I've tried to be."

Part of him wanted her to expand on that statement. Another part of him didn't. He didn't want to know if she'd been dating anyone. If she chose to try a relationship with someone else, and *not* him. Perhaps she couldn't see herself dating a former escort. A former Knight. He gritted his teeth. The job was supposed to be temporary, only until he figured out his next move. It didn't define him as a person.

Renner couldn't regret the experience. He'd met Cassie. The beautiful, sunflower-haired siren in front of him. Who'd led him here.

His new purpose.

"Turns out," she continued, transferring the bottle to her other hand. "Not everyone can make me smile the way you can."

His gaze snapped to hers. She stood on the other side of the counter, merely an arm's length away. "Have you tried?" His voice was low. Rolling through his body at the possibility.

Is she saying what I think she is?

Cassie shrugged. "It's hard to have any second dates when I'm constantly comparing them to the three we had."

His chest expanded. "You consider those dates?"

"I paid for them. Or, some of them."

"Those weren't real dates. At least, not the ones you paid for."

"What would you have called them?"

A hum echoed through Renner's body, a familiar and potent urging. "Appetizers."

The rest of her face pinked, and her lips parted. She slowly walked around the counter, and stopped directly in front of him. Mere inches away from the rumbling storm inside him. "Is there room on your camping menu for blueberry muffins?"

His heart pounded. Every part of him vibrated toward her, like gravity, at the knowledge she was free. And oh-so-willing. "Next best thing to heaven."

There's always room for muffins. And anything else you have in mind.

She set the spray bottle on the counter. "Then, why haven't you kissed me yet?"

The plum scent bombarded his senses. He could almost taste her, feel her beneath him. The dream stood in front of him, centimeters away.

Renner swallowed. "The last time I did, I ended up outside, alone in the rain."

Cassie licked her lips, which subconsciously cued him to

do the same. "There's no rain in the forecast this time." She placed her hand over his heart, electrifying his thoughts. "Just clear skies, and starry nights."

Her touch set him loose. He cradled her neck, and locked his lips to hers. Tasting, sucking, and devouring until he couldn't breathe. Renner pressed her back against the counter, his hips pushing into hers.

She wrapped her arms around him, and dug her fingers into his shoulders.

Cassie was just as delicious as he remembered. This time, more alive. More energetic, more...colorful. When she scraped her fingernails down his scalp, his dick instantly responded.

A growl rumbled low in his chest.

"I've missed you," he whispered. "Nothing's changed for me. I'm still completely in love with you." The confession lifted the weight off his heart.

She clung tighter to his neck, and slipped her knee between his legs, rubbing along his groin in just the right way. "I know," she whispered. "I love you, too."

When he mimicked her and rubbed his thigh into her pelvis, her knees buckled. He lifted her up onto the counter.

Her jade gaze locked with his, her face flushed. "*You're* the next best thing to heaven."

Epilogue

RENNER

Renner held Cassie's hand in his own, guiding her finger through the sky across the stars, outlining Orion's belt. The white-gold band on her left ring finger was as warm as her body, tucked tightly into his as they lay on a lush blanket on the beach.

Her bikini-clad ass grazed along his crotch, igniting his fire. The same fire she'd ignited since they set foot on the island.

Since he met her, really.

His wife would always ignite his soul.

My wife. The word wrapped around his brain like a delicious whiskey highball. Eternal warmth filtered through his whole body.

"That's how early travelers found their way in the world," Renner murmured in her ear. "Just from those stars. And their blind ambitions."

"Hard to imagine," Cassie murmured with a satisfied sigh. "Crossing an entire ocean not knowing what they sailed toward. How they were going to get there, or when."

He wrapped his arms around her, breathing in that delicious plum perfume and pineapple sun lotion she'd been caked in their entire honeymoon. "Much like what we're doing."

She giggled. "Hardly. We had a travel agent."

"That's not what I meant," he whispered, and slowly trailed his hand down her silky body. When he reached her thigh, he tickled her.

She screamed, and burst into laughter. As she writhed to pull away from him, Renner maneuvered himself on top of her, trapping her on either side of his arms.

Cassie gripped his hips and pulled him toward her. His rock hard length rubbed against her core, and he couldn't withhold a moan as he kissed her. Thoroughly, delectably, and under full view of the stars and heavens.

Her hum of delight vibrated in his mouth and down his sternum, awakening every nerve in his body.

She wrapped her legs around his thighs, and grabbed his ass, her nails digging into his skin in sweet torment.

"Do you want me here? Under these stars?" he whispered between kisses.

Cassie hummed her assent, arching her pelvis into him to emphasize. Then she grabbed one of the bikini strings at her hip, and gently pulled the fabric.

The crashing waves beyond the beach harmonized with the chirping of the tree frogs, signing their midnight melodies. Their own slice of heaven on a private beach away from the demands of life. One he was more than happy to return to.

Because his new life included Cassie and Landon. She had given him a new reality, one full of color and hope. Of purpose. One well worth the struggle.

With a nibble on his tongue, she reached down and rubbed his cock. Then pushed his waistband down, freeing him from his shorts. Her fingers expertly stroked him, hungry and urgent.

It was hard to imagine a moment where he wouldn't be absolutely starved for her touch. Renner pulled the strings on her other hip, and let the bathing suit fall away.

She was ready. Slick and plump, just for him.

All for him.

"You don't need the stars to find your way here," she whispered in his ear, sending sparks through his limbs. "You just need me."

He grinned. But all thought vanished when she guided his dick to her center, and pulled him in. His entire length buried inside her, and he swore through the glorious heat welcoming him home. His sac tightened, and he struggled to keep from climaxing right then.

Home. The one word occupied his otherwise liquefied mind.

Cassie would always be his home.

She'd invited him into *her* home before she even knew him. On a desperate move to cope with grief that seemed insurmountable. The precious and divine angel woke him from his hopeless and aimless existence.

To allow him to see that second chances existed. And they were worth the risk.

Her moan of pleasure melded with the ocean's waves a few yards from their feet.

Renner moved inside her, aiming for the little gasps to take its place. The signal that she'd reach her peak, and tumble with him into that comfortable numbness. Those had become his most favorite sounds.

With each plunge, her breasts jiggled, barely concealed by the shifting bikini. The temptation overwhelmed him, and he lowered his head to free a tiny pink bud, and suckle his heart's content.

Those little gasps he longed for from Cassie's lips panted in his ear, and the crashing waves grew louder.

"Tell me what it feels like."

Cheeks flushed and more beautiful than she'd ever been, her hazy gaze met his. She touched her hand to his chest, covering his heart. His pulse rammed through his body, or maybe it was hers. He couldn't tell anymore.

"Like this," she whispered. The two words were clouded with lust, a deep timbre that caressed his ears. "It feels like this was meant to be mine."

"I am," he grunted. "All of me." Renner swirled his hips

faster, and her little pants turned into higher-pitched moans that vibrated through her body and up into his.

Building, reaching, and threatening to explode. She bit her lip, and her face was completely flushed.

So full of color.

How could life be more glorious than this?

With a final plunge, her sex squeezed around him, and one long moan escaped her mouth. Cassie dug her nails into his shoulders and let her head roll back into the sand. The hottest sound in the world.

His body lost all control, and his own climax melded with hers in a fusion of souls.

I am a Knight. I cater not to just her body, but her mind and heart. Whatever she wanted was his purpose. Only for her.

A light breeze blew through the pine trees, rustling the falling oak leaves from their branches. Autumn's brilliant colors floated around Renner and Landon, as they huddled over the campfire.

The kindling lit, and finally, the flame caught hold of the wood, and spread to the rest of the logs. Sparks crackled to life, filling the evening air with pine and maple.

"I did it!" Landon's grin filled the lower half of his face. The exact same as Cassie's smile.

"Well done, champ." Renner gave him a fist-bump. "You're an expert now."

"All by myself." He grabbed a seat on an old stump, and prepped a stick with a marshmallow. "S'mores. My favorite!" With the recent haircut nearly to his scalp, he looked older than his nearly-seven-years. And with every day, he looked more and more like his father, Kyle.

He rubbed Landon's head, and kissed his forehead.

"Ugh!" He wiped his head with his arm. "Kissing is for girls!"

Renner chuckled. "When it's just you, me and Mom, it's okay, pal."

He shrugged. "Okay. But not in front of my friends."

"Oh, of course not," he mocked with a smile.

The screen door to the cabin banged shut, and Cassie appeared, carrying a tray of hot chocolates for them. Her jeans hugged her hips perfectly, and her scarlet cowl-neck sweater outlined her frame in the cozy, delicious way meant for health magazines. Her boots shuffled through a new layer of leaves, crunching beneath her soles. "Ready for the sugar overload?"

"Mommy, we made a new rule." Landon stuck his marshmallow in the flames. "No more kissing. Not around other kids."

"Oh, really?" She handed him a mug, and raised her eyebrows.

Renner threw her a wink and set the tray aside.

"But it's just us. So I can do this—," Cassie grabbed their

141

son's head and peppered kisses all over his face, "—all I want."

The kid squealed and laughed, giggles filling the camp air with love. A love that warmed Renner down to his toes.

"Daddy, help me!"

His heart stuttered.

Daddy.

Cassie's expression was just as stunned.

The boy had called him by his name ever since they'd met, and well after the wedding. He knew his real father was Kyle, and talked about him with so much pride.

"Cassie," Renner murmured, careful to keep his voice calm and positive. "Are you okay?"

She took a deep breath, and kept looking at him. But no words came out.

"He's my dad, too." Landon stood and blew out the fire that had wrapped around his marshmallow. "I have two. A daytime dad, and a nighttime one."

Cassie pulled Landon onto her lap, and gave him a hug. She helped him pull the melted, burned sugar off the stick with two graham crackers. "What's a nighttime dad, honey?"

"Daddy comes to me when I'm sleeping. He said everything will be okay. I can talk to him in my dreams. I told him all about Renner. He was happy."

Renner's heart squeezed in.

Cassie's eyes watered, which she hid by kissing Landon on the cheek.

He could tell by the way she pinched her lips together,

she couldn't get any words out.

The fire sparked again, and the smoke climbed higher among the pine trees.

Landon accidentally dropped his s'more on the ground, and gasped. Then pouted with that adorable bottom lip jutting out.

"Come here, big guy," Renner patted his leg. "I'll help you with a new one."

The little boy complied. Before long, he had another marshmallow completely charred in the flames.

Cassie watched them, silently sipping her hot chocolate.

"I'm glad you talk to your daddy in your dreams." Renner squeezed Landon's shoulder. "He can still tell you a lot of things, and watch you grow."

He shrugged, his oblivious smile focused on the sugary treat in front of him.

"Will you do me a favor?" Renner asked.

"Sure," the kid replied.

"The next time you talk to your daddy, tell him your mommy loves him very much."

Cassie smiled, her gaze glassy in the firelight locked on him.

"Okay," Landon answered.

"And that I said thanks."

His stepson frowned, his little forehead crinkling. "But he already said thanks to you."

Renner blinked, and tilted his head. "For what?"

"For making mommy smile. And making blueberry muffins with me."

Cassie's grin widened, her pearly white teeth easily visible in the shadows. After a one-shoulder shrug, she continued sipping from her mug.

Renner gave her a wink. "Making blueberry muffins with you is my favorite." He helped Landon gobble down the s'more, chocolate smearing down his chin.

The hard Marine, and former Knight escort had never imagined having a kid in his life. He didn't feel qualified. Or worthy. But little Landon had not only grown on him, he completely flipped his world upside down. He was the sweetest, most genuine thing Renner had ever seen, and a carbon copy of his mother in both heart and soul. Who knew a six-year-old could teach him how to be a loving father? All it took was a smile.

Funny, that was the same kind of thing a former Knight believed. To charm a client with only a smile. Only now he knew it's real worth.

THE END

About the
AUTHOR

Susan Sheehey writes contemporary romance, romantic suspense adventure, and romantic comedy. Water plays a crucial element in all of her novels, and she's a strong advocate for Autism awareness & acceptance. She squeezes in writing time between chauffeuring around her two boys, and guzzling down French vanilla coffee. Her beloved husband keeps her relatively sane, and full of laughter. She and her family live in Texas.

SUSAN SHEEHEY

www.SusanSheehey.com
www.bookbub.com/authors/susan-sheehey
www.amazon.com/Susan-Sheehey/e/B00EBGWXDQ
www.Facebook.com/SusanSheehey
www.Twitter.com/SusieQWriter
Join her newsletter for monthly announcements, updates,
and special giveaways on her website.

Novels By
SUSAN SHEEHEY

Stand Alone Novels
Audrey's Promise

Royals of Solana series
Prince of Solana

Jewel of Solana

Crown of Solana

Royal Wedding

Knights of Texas series
Tell Me What You Need

Tell Me What You Crave

Tell Me What You Want

Tell Me What You Feel

Sweet Escape series
Dry Spell

Hot Spell

Cold Spell

Sneak PEAK: *Tell Me What You* CRAVE

THE NEXT NOVEL IN THE KNIGHTS OF TEXAS SERIES

CHAPTER ONE

DORIAN

The hour before sunrise filled Dorian's mind with peace. The rest of the city waking up, bursting with life, just as he was headed home from a good night's work. Or, he should say a good night's *play*.

Sweet exhaustion.

Dorian *loved* mornings like this.

He strolled down the sidewalk among skyscrapers and street stalls opening for Saturday's Farmer's Market. With a yawn, he scraped his hand across the stubble on his chin. He draped his suit jacket over his shoulder, absorbing the city air. More than ready for a nightcap and his down comforter. Everything was quiet inside his high-rise's lobby. Even the doorman hadn't shown up yet.

His footsteps echoed across the marble floor on his way to check his mailbox. The elevator dinged, and the mirrored doors opened.

The curvaceous woman of his dreams, from 9C, stepped through, her cocoa brown hair elegantly piled high on her head. When she looked up from her smartphone, she stopped. The perfect rose lipstick formed a small *O*, and her glorious blue eyes widened. Then in a flicker of a heartbeat, her expression morphed into annoyance.

He reveled in the spontaneous grin he couldn't contain. "Ms. Evans. You look phenomenal, as always."

Her scowl darkened her beautiful gaze. Before she had a chance to deny him again, he cut in. "I assume you're all unpacked and settled. Since you're heading to work so early. On a Saturday morning?" Dorian glanced down her perfectly ironed blue suit, with matching knee-length, pencil skirt. Her three-inch heels were the same color as her mauve nails. She was always so put together, but in a way that seemed effortless.

Grace's jaw twitched. "You're returning extremely late from your *date*, Mr. West. Or should I presume you've already been home since I saw you leave last night? In the same suit."

He sighed with a smile. "I love that you pay attention to

my details." Then he shrugged. "But the bills have to be paid. And you're one to accuse me of loving my job too much. You came home from yours so late last night, and now you're back out in less than..." He checked his silver A.Lange & Sohne watch. "Seven hours."

Her scowl disappeared instantly. To become a completely blank expression. The change so sudden, he almost stopped breathing. Or maybe it was from her delectable lips pressing together, and smudging the lipstick in the corner of her mouth.

It took everything he had not to reach out and wipe it away.

"Please, Grace. Just one coffee. That's all I ask. You won't regret it."

"Yes, I'm sure you've perfected your speed dating pitch, Mr. West. Excuse me." She brushed past him.

Her spicy perfume with a hint of floral overtones almost knocked his senses sideways. With every click of her heels on the floor, her scent faded.

His chest ached the more it dwindled.

An envelope fell from under her arm and slid across the floor. Dorian couldn't even tell she'd had something tucked there. He craved to discover more secrets of her body. Even more...what went on inside that gorgeous head of hers. Her expressions always betrayed her silence.

"Ms. Evans?"

She stopped and turned.

He picked up the envelope, noticing the handwritten address, from someone in Frisco, Texas. Only twenty-minutes away.

Grace grabbed it and pulled, but he didn't let go. Her slate-blue eyes met his.

Her slow and deep intake of breath made him imagine the kind of slow and deep pleasure she'd have under his touch. The image stirred in his mind, and mirrored in his pants.

"Mr. West, did it ever occur to you I'm too old to play your games?"

He blinked. *Too old?*

"Set your aspirations to someone more your age—"

"How old do you think I—"

"Or someone more fitting to your...lifestyle."

His bit the inside of his cheek. This wasn't the first time a woman disapproved of his profession. It was the first time he felt the need to defend himself. "Does my occupation offend you?"

Her nostrils flared. "Good day. Or should I say, good night."

"Try my name. Just once." Dorian threw her a wink.

Grace studied him for a minute, until she finally left.

He smiled. She hadn't frowned at him again. *Chiseling away the ice, little by little.*

CPSIA information can be obtained
at www.ICGtesting.com
Printed in the USA
LVHW101248300323
742972LV00005B/508

9 781947 874022